Praise for Emma Lang's
Endless Heart

"...this is a very well-written and entertaining historical Western romance."

~ *Library Journal*

"I don't know what it is about an Emma Lang story but I am so glad to read and review the latest in the Heart series."

~ *Guilty Pleasures Book Reviews*

"This is a great historical western romance with every element that you could possibly want... And, in the end, it was perfect."

~ *Night Owl Reviews*

"*Endless Heart* is about kindness, forgiveness and love—a heady mix that drew me in from page one. Lang delivers a highly emotional story with characters you just have to love.."

~ *Book Lovers Inc.*

"I loved *Endless Heart*. It's a gritty and honest story with two people who have their issues. This is a true Beth Williamson story, told the only way she can, with humor and affection for each character."

~ *Book Obsessed Chicks*

Look for these titles by
Beth Williamson

Now Available:

Marielle's Marshal

Branded

Hell for Leather

Private Lives

On His Knees

The Malloy Family

The Bounty

The Prize

The Reward

The Treasure

The Gift

The Tribute

The Legacy

The Devils on Horseback

Nate

Jake

Zeke

Lee

Gideon

Print Anthologies

Midsummer Night's Steam:
Sand, Sun and Sex

Leather and Lace

Secret Thoughts

Endless Heart

Beth Williamson
writing as Emma Lang

SAMHAIN
PUBLISHING

Samhain Publishing, Ltd.
11821 Mason Montgomery Road, 4B
Cincinnati, OH 45249
www.samhainpublishing.com

Endless Heart
Copyright © 2013 by Beth Williamson
Print ISBN: 978-1-61921-056-1
Digital ISBN: 978-1-60928-955-3

Editing by Sasha Knight
Cover by Scott Carpenter

This book is a work of fiction. The names, characters, places, and incidents are products of the writer's imagination or have been used fictitiously and are not to be construed as real. Any resemblance to persons, living or dead, actual events, locale or organizations is entirely coincidental.

First Samhain Publishing, Ltd. electronic publication: May 2012
First Samhain Publishing, Ltd. print publication: April 2013

Dedication

This book is dedicated to all of us who have made mistakes, who have felt the pain of our own shortcomings and the pinch of being unable to forgive ourselves. It's not who we were or what we did, it's who we are and what we do.

Chapter One

June 1873

Forestville, Wyoming

Lettie Brown stared down at the man at her feet and resisted the urge to kick him. The stench of vomit wafted up, and she felt the vile liquid seeping into her shoes.

"Mister, wake up." She pushed at his shoulder with her shin. It was the best she could do considering he'd landed smack-dab on her feet just inside the door of the restaurant.

The man with the snarled, dirty, molasses-colored hair didn't move an inch. Lettie looked behind her into the shadowed building. At five in the morning, the Blue Plate was empty of customers and staff. She had arrived early to meet the freight wagon and instead it had brought her a filthy vagabond who puked on her.

"Wake up." She reached down and shook his shoulder. "I ain't gonna stand here all day while you ruin my only pair of shoes."

Still no response. She hitched up her skirt and bent down, loathe to put her hands on the man, but there wasn't any other choice. His hair was crusted with something she didn't want to be privy to, and it was too long and shaggy. All over his cheeks he had bruises and cuts, which looked like they would fester soon. A gash on his forehead bled profusely.

She lightly tapped his face, her gut telling her no one with that many wounds needed to be hit again. Lettie knew that firsthand.

"Mister?"

His eyes popped open, startling a yelp out of her. They were the color of smoke and ashes. She'd never seen such a thing before.

"Violet?" He sounded as though he'd been chewing on rocks. His eyes fluttered closed, and he went limp.

Lettie almost exploded right then and there. He'd called her by her given name, one she hadn't used since she was ten years old. Who was this man? And how did he know who she was? Josiah was dead, no longer able to hurt her, but someone must have sent this man here to find her. Her heart pounded hard enough to make her teeth rattle. "Damn."

"Lettie, what is happening?" Marta Gunderson appeared on the stairs that led to the rooms above the restaurant. She wore her nightclothes and a cap with her blonde and gray hair sticking out every which way beneath it. She and her husband Pieter, both German immigrants, ran the restaurant together.

"I was heading outside to ask the freight wagon driver to pull around the back when this man fell inside and landed on my feet." Lettie frowned at the stranger who had turned her life inside out with one word, not to mention ruined her shoes.

Marta peered at the stranger and tsked. "Ah, *liebchen,* we must be kind to strangers, ya? Let me get Pieter and we bring him upstairs. The poor man has wounds to be tended to." She turned and went back upstairs much quicker than a sixty-year-old woman should then called back downstairs. "Heat some water, Lettie."

Lettie pushed at the stranger's shoulder until he rolled onto his back, freeing her feet. The puddle of vomit was more like bile, telling her the man hadn't had a real meal in some time. Judging by the smell his meals had been liquid, a cheap rotgut no doubt.

She pulled off her shoes and padded in her stocking feet to the kitchen, leaving the man lying in the doorway alone. Certainly nothing worse could happen to him there. She stoked up the embers in the big stove until they glowed brightly, then put in kindling to get the fire going. After pumping a bucketful of water and putting it on the stove, she set to work cleaning her shoes. The chore gave her a few minutes to calm her racing heart. She was jumping to conclusions. There were plenty of women named Violet. The man probably had a wife with the same name, or maybe a sister.

He was no threat to her, couldn't possibly be.

"Who's the dead man?" Eleven-year-old Dennis Fox peeked in the kitchen door, his brown hair tousled and expression wary. His mother, Karen, was a waitress at the restaurant while he did odd jobs for extra coin each week.

"He's not dead."

"Are you sure? He smells like he's dead."

Lettie hid a shaky smirk at the boy's bald honesty. "Nah, he's just hurt."

"Mrs. Gunderson upstairs?" He glanced around the kitchen. "She wanted me to sweep the porch before school."

"Go ahead and get to sweeping then. She'll be nursing the dead man and won't have time to jaw about your chores." Lettie watched the boy's face as he swallowed, his eyes wide. She never could speak to children proper, so she kept to her usual blunt way. Unfortunately, her way didn't work, but she didn't know what else to do.

Dennis opened his mouth then closed it without speaking and disappeared back through the door with only a whisper of sound. She didn't mean to be abrupt or scare him, but she also didn't want him to stay in the kitchen. Lettie knew what was coming, and she was helpless to prevent it. She needed to be

11

alone to gather her wits.

Life hadn't been kind to her. After the monster she'd married was killed, Lettie allowed herself to pursue what she thought was a normal life. The last six months were the only time she could remember feeling content. Not happy, but definitely content. Forestville had given her a chance, and she was finally taking advantage of it. Her work at the restaurant helped her survive, and her work at the newspaper gave her a purpose. Life was almost normal.

Until this morning. Until the dirty stranger crashed into the restaurant. He had brought an element of pain and a crush of memories she had locked away last year.

Violet.

Against her will, her hands shook and a buzzing sounded in her head. She hung on to the edge of the wooden sink, gripping it tight enough to make her knuckles pop. Dark memories crowded her thoughts, stealing her control. She bent at the waist until her head was level with the sink. It had been so long since she'd had an attack, she had tried to forget about them. Yet here one was, ready to send her into a tailspin of shadows.

Lettie slid to the floor and crawled to the corner, heart galloping, eyes burning and stomach churning. She couldn't catch her breath. Squeezing into the niche, she pulled up her knees and pressed her head down.

I'm safe. I'm safe. No one is here to hurt me. I'm safe. I'm safe.

She started rocking, desperately trying to get hold of herself. If she didn't, the screaming, the howling and the weeping would commence. It would take days to shake off the darkness. Coldness seeped through her, raising gooseflesh and shivers.

"Lettie?" A soft, cool hand pressed against her neck. "Oh, sweetheart, I'm sorry." Her best friend, Angeline Carver, squatted beside her. "Dennis came and got me. Told me about the dead man. I came over as fast as I could."

Lettie didn't open her eyes, her hands balled into fists while she fought against her demons. Any second, something was going to explode from her chest.

Be strong, Lettie. Be strong.

Angeline squeezed in beside her and put her arm around Lettie's shoulders. "It's okay, I'm here." Her presence, the warmth and kindness she had in abundance, threw its cloak around Lettie like a blanket. "I won't let anyone hurt you."

Tears stung Lettie's eyes, but she would not open them. She would not let them fall from her eyes no matter how long it took for them to go away. After that bastard Josiah died last year, she'd promised herself she would never cry over a man again. Ever. Lettie aimed to keep that promise come hell or high water.

Angeline murmured to her while she rubbed Lettie's back. By the time burbling noises echoed from the water on the stove, the panic had begun to subside, and she opened her eyes. She was able to unlock her hands, glad to see her nails hadn't cut into her palms this time. The tiny crescent scars there spoke of darker times.

"What happened?" Angeline whispered.

Lettie shook her head. "Nothing. It's stupid."

"No, it's not. Something set you down, and I want to know what." Angeline was truly angelic looking with her blonde hair and blue eyes, but she was fierce beneath the sweet exterior. "Sam and I told you when we married you are part of our family. We protect each other, remember?"

Blissfully happy in their new marriage, the couple had

taken Lettie in, giving her the first real home she'd ever had. The house was large enough for three and had all the room she needed to be comfortable. Then the couple had moved into a big house by the lake, leaving Lettie alone in a house that wasn't hers.

Angeline had never stopped taking care of Lettie even when they weren't living together. Folks may have thought it was the other way around, that Lettie was the caretaker, but they'd be wrong. Angeline was the reason they had left Utah, escaped the monster and embarked on a new life. After five years of living hell, Lettie hadn't had the courage to break free.

Angeline had helped to loosen the knot of fear and panic that lived inside Lettie. She was truly blessed to have such a friend in her life. She had so much to be grateful for. If only she could find the strength to stop being afraid of everything.

"There is a man in the restaurant."

"Did he hurt you?" A pinch of anger colored Angeline's question.

"No, nothing like that. He's been hurt, beat all to hell and back. He stumbled in off the freight wagon, fell onto my feet and puked on my shoes." Saying it out loud made it sound silly, not worthy of what she had gone through. However, nothing would make the experience disappear. The tang of fear and self-loathing coated her tongue. She couldn't tell her friend about the man saying her name. Maybe Lettie had dreamed it and it wasn't worth mentioning.

"I wondered why your shoes were in the sink." Angeline squeezed her shoulders. "I'm sorry that happened."

"It was bad luck I was there."

"No, that's not what I meant." Angeline leaned closer. "I'm sorry it made you remember and get scared. I'm sorry you had to go through it again."

14

Lettie took a deep breath and looked at her friend. Angeline's expression of worry and love chased away the last of the demons clawing at Lettie's soul. She took Angeline's hand and gripped it tight. Words crowded in Lettie's throat.

"I, um... That is, I—"

"You're welcome." Angeline got to her feet and shook her blue skirt. She held out her hand to Lettie. "I'm guessing Mrs. Gunderson is waiting on the water?"

Lettie accepted the help up although she was twice her friend's size. When she stood, the heat from the stove warmed her back. She would be okay, thanks to Angeline.

"Yep. She's got it in her head to heal the stranger. Did I mention he also smells like cheap whiskey?"

Shane Murphy was no longer a man. He accepted it even if it tasted like poison on his tongue. The bald truth was always bitter, or in this case, deadly. He'd been too much of a coward to find a way not to live his miserable existence.

"For pity's sake, mister, would you stop fighting me?" The bottom of the worst pit in hell was apparently inhabited by a witch who liked to beat him. Her voice cut through the fading haze of drink. She sounded almost human, although she screeched and howled at him, kicking and slapping him. He tried to hide from her but couldn't make his legs move. To his shame, tears burned his eyes and his throat ached with a pitiful helplessness.

Ten years ago when he'd been a twenty-year-old fool, he would have fought harder. Today he gave in quickly, cowered, beaten and shamed by his own inaction.

Shane managed to pull open his eyes although he would

swear ten-pound weights sat on his lids. The brightness of the room slammed into his naked eyeballs, and he cringed in agony. A brown-haired witch hovered over him, her wings scaly masses of dark feathers. His skull pounded with a whooshing sound, each pulse pure pain. Perhaps the witch had been kicking him in the head. Of course, the tiny bit of him that still functioned recognized that ache as lack of whiskey, a condition he avoided for as long as possible. Lately, that had included two months of continuous drink with nary a pause between bottles. Until now.

"I swear to you if you don't stop, I will smack you." The witch grabbed at his arms, and he pulled away from her grip. "Dammit!"

"Language, *liebchen*." The second voice sounded like an angel or a grandmother, someone safe and sweet. "He does not know what he is doing. He is hurt."

The witch snorted. "He ain't hurt, Marta. He's coming off the drink and being ornery."

Oh the witch was smart, very smart indeed. She knew his secret already, although it wasn't much of a secret. Her kind probably knew things without asking a question. Shane was leery about looking at her, not that his eyes were working proper anyway.

"Still we should be kind. The world depends on kindness." The angel grandmother was the voice of reason. She would protect him from the witch.

"If you want me to doctor his wounds, I need to be able to clean them first. If he keeps fighting me, I'm going back downstairs."

Shane realized two things at once. The warmth he'd attributed to her breath was actually a cloth on his forehead, which was currently dripping water down his cheek. The second was that he was lying in a soft bed for the first time in at least three years.

The fight went out of him in a blink. His whiskey-induced haze had reduced him to a blathering fool, a wounded one who pushed away the people who were trying to help him. Shane didn't deserve their kindness, but they couldn't know that.

He managed to keep one eye open and saw the outlines of two women, one on either side of him. The witch did have brown hair and brown clothes, like a bird of prey. The other one shone like a white light in the sunshine, too bright to focus on. They were women, not strange things like witches and angels. Whiskey had destroyed more than his stomach, it had pickled his mind too.

"Sorry," he mumbled, his voice rusty and thick.

"Did he say something?" The witch squeezed the rag, and water sluiced into his eye.

"Ow, that hurts."

"Mister, you got a lot more problems than water in your eye." She was ruthless, this witch, wiping his face with a rag that seemed to be made of scrub brush. It scraped his skin, sending shards of pain through him, joining the already excruciating agony of his head. He closed his eyes, trying to keep the roar down to a minimum.

"I think he fell back to sleep," the angel said.

"Or he's unconscious again." The witch kept wiping his face, this time with more vigor, as though she had free rein to abuse him while he slept. He didn't have the wherewithal to do anything but endure. "This one needs stitches. It won't stop bleeding."

He was bleeding? Why was he bleeding?

"Does that look like a boot mark to you?" The witch's voice

had changed, sliding lower. He heard a new tone, something that sounded suspiciously like anger.

"The poor man. Someone has shown him nothing but unkindness." The angel grandmother's cool touch skimmed across his skin. "And his hands are, *ach.* His fingers are broken."

Shock rippled through him. It appeared someone, not likely these two women even if one of them was a witch, had beaten him. The truly sad thing was he had no idea who had done it or how it had happened.

He hoped they didn't ask him.

"It's good he's asleep. The pain won't be as bad." The witch's murmur was nearly tender, and he almost forgot what she'd done to hurt him under the guise of helping him.

Then she yanked on his fingers, which was followed by a sickening crunch of bone on bone. He howled in agony as the pain radiated up his arm. The last thing he remembered was swinging wildly with his other hand, and everything went black.

Lettie stared at her reflection in the small looking glass, focusing on the bruise currently forming on her jaw and cheek. She didn't have a mirror, hadn't ever had one, but Alice did. The young woman lived above the restaurant and worked as a waitress. Alice had never experienced an ounce of real pain in her life. The silly thing was quite in love with herself. She certainly primped enough each day before serving food.

In contrast, Lettie rarely wanted to look in a mirror. She knew she wasn't pretty, but that didn't matter to her. What scared her was the possibility of what she would see in her eyes—the gaping maw of nothing that inhabited her soul. The one thing she couldn't change in her new life was her heart, which had been torn asunder so long ago.

But now that man, the stranger who'd puked on her shoes, had changed everything. His actions forced her to use a looking glass for the first time in at least ten years. Was there nothing he wasn't going to corrupt? She assumed he hadn't meant to punch her. After all, she had been resetting his broken fingers. Yet it seemed everything he touched became a problem or a pain for her.

She wanted him to leave. Now. It didn't matter that his face was almost in pieces or that his fingers had been bent backwards or that someone had kicked his head repeatedly. He disrupted her existence and her peace, something she had worked hard to achieve. For that, she needed him to move on.

Marta would never allow it of course. The kind-hearted woman had taken Lettie and Angeline in, and Lettie had been a nightmare a year earlier. She still carried a knife even though it had been months since the threat to her had been eliminated. The presence of the blade tucked into a sheath on her thigh gave her comfort.

Most days she was content with her lot in life, never expecting more. That path included disappointment and pain. No, she was glad to stay put as a waitress and part-time newspaper publisher. Perhaps one day she might write an article for the publication. For now, Angeline's husband Sam wrote the articles and Lettie did the printing. It was a soothing chore to use the press, the smell of the ink and paper a familiar companion.

Standing in Alice's room, Lettie was uncomfortable and angry. She poured water in the basin and quickly scrubbed away the blood staining her fingers as best she could. The coppery smell had made her stomach roil the entire time she'd been stitching the man's head wound. It wasn't a perfect doctoring, but at least the bleeding had stopped. That meant he could get better and leave.

"Why are you in my room, Lettie?" Alice asked from the doorway.

"I needed to wash up. Marta told me to come in here." Lettie dried her hands on her apron and picked up the basin. "I'll toss this, and you can forget I was here."

Alice stopped her with a hand on Lettie's arm, her blue eyes full of concern. "What happened to your face?"

"My face has been crooked for years. Another lump isn't going to change things awful much." In fact, her nose leaned to the left and one cheekbone was larger than the other. There wasn't much about her face to ruin.

"You shouldn't put yourself down so much. There is nothing wrong with your face." Alice sounded sincere, another surprise. "Who hit you?"

Lettie didn't need to have another person concerned about her or her well-being. "Nobody. It's nothing, and it sure ain't your business." Pushing past the sputtering young woman, Lettie escaped from the room.

She sucked in a deep breath and walked to the window at the end of the hallway. Alice's footsteps echoed from the stairs as she went down into the restaurant. Later on, she would probably have a few words for Lettie about the encounter, but she didn't care. It wouldn't change a thing.

After throwing the pink-tinged water out into the deserted backyard, she set the basin at the door to Alice's room and headed toward the stairs. As her foot landed on the top step, a small moan came from the other room. The room she used to sleep in. The room that held the stranger.

Her head told her to keep walking, not to stop to check on him. It had been fifteen minutes since they finished cleaning him up and bandaging his wounds. Marta had gone downstairs to make biscuits, fussing about how the fluffy concoctions would be late for the breakfast crowd.

There was no one to help him but Lettie. If she were a stronger woman, she would have walked back in there and seen to him. If she were a stronger woman, she wouldn't have hesitated. People thought she was tough, but they were wrong. She had run, had hidden from her fears for so long, she didn't know how to face them. Lettie used anger to keep others at a distance and her own cowardice to stay there.

Lettie walked downstairs with his moan echoing in her ears and her cheek still throbbing from his fist. She set aside her guilt, smashing it down deep into her heart. Unfortunately, she had a conscience that lived outside her body.

Marta stood near the bottom of the steps, flour covering her hands and wrists, along with a few smudges on her chin. "How is the patient?"

Lettie couldn't lie to the woman who had helped save her. "I didn't look in on him."

Marta's expression fell, the corners of her mouth drooping. "He didn't mean to hurt you, *liebchen*."

"I know, but I just...well...I couldn't." Lettie could hardly put into words what she felt or why she felt it. The jumbled stew churning inside her had no rhyme or reason. She listened to her gut and tried to make the best choices. Things didn't always end up the way she wanted, but she knew no other way to sort through it all.

"You must. I have to cook and bake. With Angeline not here, there is no one else." Marta's sad expression was almost comical given the amount of flour covering her. "We are nothing if we are not kind."

Lettie knew she shouldn't be such a fool about taking care

of another human being in need. It wasn't as though she didn't feel for him. On the contrary, she felt too much when she was around him. Yet she didn't want to disappoint Marta.

"I will go check on him, but I can't sit with him. Please don't ask me to." Her words shook as they rolled off her tongue, like they were perched on top of a teetering tower, ready to fall to the ground and break into a thousand pieces.

"Is good, is good." Marta patted her cheek, no doubt leaving smears of flour and dough. "Alice and Karen will serve the customers this morning. You stay upstairs and check on him every ten minutes."

With that, the older woman turned and walked back toward the kitchen. Lettie had gotten herself into a situation she didn't want to be in. She had no choice but to help the stranger. If he hit her again, she would hit him back. Although she was afraid of her own shadow, she would never allow anyone to hit her if she could stop them. She would let the first punch pass since he was out of his mind from blood loss and pain. However, she would never allow him to hurt her again.

Never.

Shane woke slowly this time. The roaring in his head had subsided somewhat, but that didn't mean the rest of his body wasn't moaning. The whiskey had well and truly worn off, leaving him in a puddle of exactly what he'd been avoiding—pain. He vaguely remembered his fingers had been broken, and someone had stitched up his forehead. There had been a brown witch and a granny angel, or perhaps it was the imaginings of drink.

"I know you're awake. I can tell because your breathing changed." Like it or not, the sharp voice yanked him fully into consciousness.

When he attempted to move, agony sliced through him like a sharp knife. Every bit of him hurt. Was his entire body broken?

"I'm only going to be in here another minute, so you best get to talking, mister."

He tried to open both eyes, but he couldn't get the left one to budge. It was swollen shut. The right one worked well enough, but it burned like hell from the bright sunshine in the room. He blinked to clear away the stinging and finally focused on the woman standing beside the bed.

It was the witch.

She had brown hair, brown eyes and brown clothes, like a brown bird that lived in a brown house and ate brown food. She was somber all over except for her eyes, which reflected anger and pain—two things he knew well enough to recognize in a glance. To his surprise, she also had a shiner. Her left cheek and eye were red and purple, as though the bruise was still forming. His stomach flipped at the memory of swinging his fist.

"Did I do that?" he managed to croak.

Her hand flew to her eye, and she touched it with her fingertips. "It makes no never mind. You were out of your head."

Her words said one thing, but her expression said if he did it again, she'd likely pound on him. Shane was embarrassed to think he had punched a woman, especially one who was taking care of a stranger.

"I'm sorry for it. I, uh, don't hit women." He winced at the idiocy that came out of his mouth. "Thank you for taking care of me. I'll be out of here shortly." He told himself to stand up but found his limbs would not obey. He could only lift one arm with monumental effort. "Or maybe in another hour."

She pursed her lips and raised her right brow. "I don't think you'll be sitting up for another three days, if you're lucky. Somebody beat the stuffing out of you, mister, from stem to stern."

Somebody *beat* him? That would explain the overall inability to move as well as the pain coursing through him. He searched his mind for a glimmer of a memory. He remembered a freight wagon pulling out of Cheyenne. He couldn't recall much of anything else until this woman appeared in his life. The rest was a black void. Hell he didn't know where he was or what day it was.

"How did I get here? And where is here?"

She sighed and sat on the chair next to the bed, careful to keep a three-foot distance from him. "I owe you that much, I guess. This is Forestville, Wyoming, and you're at the Blue Plate Diner. We're upstairs in one of the bedrooms. The owner's wife, Marta, insisted on doctoring you."

The woman clearly did not want to be there taking care of him, not that he blamed her. After all, he had punched her. He peered around at the room, wondering whose it was, possibly the woman sitting beside the bed. An odd sensation shimmied down his spine at the thought. He shook it away with effort.

"What day is it?"

She didn't look surprised at the question. "It's Saturday, June twenty-first."

Shane's stomach dropped to his knees. He had lost *three* weeks. *Three* weeks. Another memory flickered to life. He'd been jawing with a patron in a saloon about it being the first of June. There had been rotgut and talk of riding in a freight wagon, earning his keep by helping to load and unload. He started shaking all over.

Sweet Jesus, he had kept himself in a drunken stupor for

long periods before, but not for three weeks. Bile crept up his throat, and he glanced around for a chamber pot or basin. His unwilling nurse grabbed a pot from beneath the bed and held it at the ready. He managed to lean over the side of the bed and vomit into the container. There was next to nothing in his stomach, but it burned his throat and mouth. No doubt he hadn't eaten in days.

"At least you're not puking on my shoes again."

He wanted to ask what she meant, but his stomach heaved once more. Stars swam behind his eyes as his body convulsed, forcing him to vomit nothing but acid from his churning gut. A cold cloth landed on the back of his neck, and its presence relaxed the muscles there. Within minutes, the urge to vomit passed and he was able to lay back. She used the cold cloth to wipe his face and mouth as though he were an infant. His hands were bandaged, and he couldn't clean himself up, but that fact didn't matter.

Shane was worthless at that moment. Completely, utterly worthless.

"I'll be right back." Her footsteps echoed as she walked out of the room, leaving him to struggle alone.

He managed not to cry or howl, although it took a lot of effort to contain the sounds of his agony and self-hatred. Shane Murphy had hit bottom, the very dregs of nowhere. He had the choice to stay there or find a way to get back on his feet. A creak of wood startled him. He forced his eye open to find the woman back in the chair. Had he passed out?

She held his gaze, not flinching from the pitiful mess he was. She had grit. "Now that you've got that out of the way, what's your name?"

"Shane Murphy."

"Where do you hail from, Mr. Murphy?"

"Missouri."

"Long way from home." She folded her arms, pushing up her breasts, and to his complete surprise, he found his gaze straying to them. They were large and round, more than enough for any man.

What the hell was he thinking?

"I, um, wandered a bit after the war."

"It's been eight years since the war ended, Mr. Murphy. That's a lot of wandering." She acted like a general interrogating a prisoner.

"I don't think I need to explain my life to you, ma'am." He wouldn't have normally gotten his back up at her methods, but damned if she didn't make him feel as ornery as she was.

"Fair enough." Her gaze roamed over his face. "But if I was you, I'd want to make sure I didn't end up near death on a stranger's doorstep again."

Her blunt jab hurt like a bitch when it hit. She definitely had no compunction about being brutally honest, did she?

"What's your name?"

She started then frowned at him. "Lett—I mean Miss Brown."

If he had an ounce of energy, he might have laughed at the fact this woman sheathed in brown was aptly named after the color she swam in. "Miss Brown, I want to thank you for helping a fella like me. I know I likely stink—"

"Understatement."

He forged on, annoyed but determined to speak his peace. "And I ain't a pretty sight right now, but I do appreciate you helping me. It's a kind thing to do."

"We are nothing if we aren't kind." Her words were hollow, recited as though they had been drilled into her. He didn't know and couldn't guess what she was feeling, but it surely wasn't kindness.

"Well, um, thank you." Sweat rolled down the side of his face as the shaking grew worse. He was thirsty, but more than that, he needed a drink. A whole lot. More than he'd ever needed anything in his life. That was a lie, but at that moment he had to accept it as truth.

She peered at him. "You're feeling poorly because you're coming off the whiskey."

It wasn't a question, and he didn't feel obligated to answer. Instead he closed his working eye and focused on something, anything, to stop the urge to crawl out of the room to find a saloon.

"I'm thirsty."

"I can offer you water or coffee, Mr. Murphy. There's no whiskey in this restaurant." She got to her feet.

The last thing he wanted to do was be alone. That would make things much worse. Although Miss Brown wasn't a demure, soft-spoken woman, she was better than his own company.

"Coffee would be good. You'll come back?" He hated the pitiful note in his voice, evidence of the puling idiot who inhabited his body nowadays.

A small sigh escaped her. "I suppose. I do have a job, and I ain't getting paid for sitting with you." She left the room with her back ramrod straight and her arms at her sides.

He should feel guilty, but he didn't. Shane had become selfish, and right about then, it served him well. All he felt was relief that he wouldn't have to stare at the cheery lace curtains and clean walls, in the soft bed, and know he didn't belong there. He didn't belong anywhere except hell, which had taken up residence inside him, traveled with him, haunted his

27

nightmares and kept him awash in whiskey.

Until now. Until he ran into the estimable Miss Brown and her severe brown ways. She might be an unlikely nurse and companion, but he didn't need sympathy. He needed someone who would treat him as he needed to be treated, as nobody.

As the minutes ticked by and she did not return, Shane dozed. Dark images and shadows surrounded him. He fought against them but he had no strength. The bed became a doorway into hell, one that beckoned him. It was a trap. It had to be a trap, one to punish him for the wrongdoings he'd committed. There were so, so many of them.

He struggled against the bed, trying to save himself, although he was tempted to give in to the pull and let himself finally be free. Yet a piece of him—he wanted to believe it was the part of the man left inside him—prodded him to fight for his life.

Shane heaved himself out of bed and landed face down on the floor. Through the pain, he grimaced in triumph. He probably looked like a monster, but it didn't matter a whit. He crawled toward the door.

Shane.

He stopped in mid-motion, his ears straining to hear it again, his heart pounding. Miss Brown hadn't come back, he was alone in the room, and he had no idea who had called his name.

You're mine, Shane. Where do you think you're going?

Now he recognized the voice, and the confusion turned to full-blown panic. Violet was dead and gone. She couldn't be there, taunting him, calling him. He scrambled for the door, rowing against an unseen current, his hands screeching in agony as he slammed them into the wooden floor.

He had to escape.

Lettie stared out the kitchen window at the morning sunshine. Bits of dust and flowers floated in the sunbeams streaming into the yard. Somewhere a dog barked, and Marta hummed as she retrieved another batch of biscuits from the big black stove.

The fresh pot of coffee wasn't ready yet, and it gave Lettie a convenient excuse to stay downstairs, away from Shane Murphy, for a few extra minutes. He'd looked awful, as though he'd been put into a coffee bean grinder and spat out the other side. With one eye swollen shut, cuts, bruises and stitches covering every inch of his visage, he was almost monstrous.

She couldn't even peek at the rest of him. His face was enough to make her want to vomit right alongside him. Lettie had been him once, barely able to move, her mouth so sore she couldn't do anything but dribble broth through her lips. His very presence brought back painful memories. She had to work hard to keep them at bay.

"The coffee is ready," Marta prompted. "Be careful carrying it upstairs so you don't burn yourself."

Lettie could have told her that burning herself was the smallest of her concerns. At least that would be a real injury, not one lying in wait like a nightmare to pounce on her. She took her time filling two of the large mugs, then added a spoon of sugar to hers. He could drink it black.

"You are a good girl, *liebchen.*" Marta smiled at her. The genuine affection in her gaze gave Lettie pause. She had been blessed to find such lovely people, a family, to become a part of. Some days the darkness beat away the light she'd been living in, but Marta's gentle, loving ways always reminded Lettie of what she had.

"No, you are a good person, Marta." Lettie set the mugs on

the small table and pulled the startled older woman into a hug. Generally, Lettie touched no one, and no one, except Angeline, touched her. "Thank you for everything."

Before she turned into a complete idiot, Lettie retrieved the cups and escaped from the kitchen, not daring to look at Marta's expression. The hug was a surprise to both of them, and Lettie needed time to figure out exactly why she'd done it. Touching others gave her hives, and she had a strict rule against it. Now she'd gone off and hugged the woman who had become her mother, of sorts, as though it was an everyday occurrence.

Taking care of Mr. Murphy was turning her into a fool, or maybe the punch to her face had jumbled up her mind enough that she was acting loco. Either way, the strangeness had begun with the man in the bed upstairs.

A thump from above made her stop in mid-stride.

She turned to see Karen and Alice, who were currently serving customers, look at her. The waitresses both had their eyebrows raised. If Lettie knew Karen, the thirty-five-year-old was already quizzing Marta about Mr. Murphy, as she was always on the prowl for a new husband. Alice was nosy and too immature to know her elbow from her ear.

Lettie shrugged at them and continued up, trepidation growing with each step. The upstairs was dead quiet, the only noise the low murmur from the restaurant below. The door to the room where the stranger lay was closed. She had distinctly left it open knowing she would be carrying coffee up. So who had closed it? She set the mugs on the floor beside the door and wiped her hands on her apron.

After taking a deep breath, she put her hand on the knob, half-expecting it not to turn. However, it moved easily, and the door swung open.

The bed was empty.

Surprised couldn't describe what she felt. The man couldn't sit up fifteen minutes ago. Where was he? She swung around as though someone was standing behind her, but the hallway was empty, the rest of the bedroom doors open. A small sound came from the corner of the room.

She peeked around the door, heart in her throat, bladder threatening to let loose. There sat Mr. Murphy, his naked back gleaming in the sun, curled into a ball, his arms around his head, knees up. The position was so achingly familiar, her annoyance and fear vanished. She knew what it was to be flat-out terrified. For the first time in a very long time, Lettie was the one who could help.

Normally the recipient of assistance, she hadn't reached out to another human being to offer anything but a plate of food in at least six years. The stranger roused the sleeping conscience within her, the one beaten into submission by hard fists. She closed the door and got to her knees in front of him, trying not to startle him. He wore his drawers only, and a pitiful pair they were.

"Mr. Murphy?" She kept her voice low.

He made a sound deep in his throat, a part-growl, part-whimper, and tried to make himself smaller. Shane was a big man, and it seemed impossible he could be any tinier than he was, but he managed it. Lettie slid up beside him, as Angeline had done for her so many times, and lowered her arm until it touched his bare shoulders. His skin was cool and clammy. She told herself not to pull away—he needed her. Right now that was more important than following her no-touching rule.

"I'm here now. I won't let anyone hurt you."

He shuddered at the contact, but he didn't push her away or protest. She let her arm relax until it was across his back—

his very wide back. She could barely reach his other shoulder. He trembled so hard it made her bones rattle. Lettie conjured Angeline's strength and found herself talking in soothing tones, her body heat warming his chilled flesh.

"I'm sorry, Violet. So sorry."

Her name, *again*, from his lips. Her stomach clenched, sending the taste of bile into her throat. She nearly ran from the room. There had to be a logical explanation. Obviously there had been someone named Violet in his life and he was apologizing to her. There was no chance he knew Lettie's first name or the shortened version of it she used now.

"It's okay, Shane." She rubbed his back. Being close to him and providing comfort made her feel awkward and unnerved. "I, uh, forgive you."

He turned his head and snuggled against her until her chin rested on his hair, which stank to high heaven. She couldn't pull away now. The man needed her no matter how uneasy she was.

"I ain't never been the husband you needed. I'm sorry, so sorry," he mumbled against her neck. It appeared Violet was his wife, and Shane suffered guilt over something he'd done.

"Shhhh, it's okay. You're safe now. I won't let anyone hurt you." Lettie repeated herself over and over in a singsong pattern. It wasn't the words, it was the tone. She knew that firsthand.

Ten minutes passed, and she realized he had calmed because of her ministrations. He'd relaxed so much he'd fallen asleep.

Well, wasn't this a predicament. Here she was all cozy with a stranger, who was bloody, reeked and only wearing his drawers. Lettie wanted to run from the room like her ass was on fire, yet she stayed, strangely gratified to be able to console him.

Chapter Two

Lettie walked home slowly, her mind and her gut awhirl. The sun had dropped low in the sky, painting the way for her in orange and pink. The day had taken a wrong turn somewhere, as though it had been part of a dream. Shane Murphy's presence in her life had twisted everything sideways.

Emotions and thoughts she hadn't permitted now rolled through her. Heck, they rolled over her. She felt as though she'd been in a fight, exhausted and quivering. The memory of the unusual moment when she'd been in the corner with him made her heart flutter each time she thought of it.

Nothing like that had happened to her before—nothing. Helping him, being the person to give comfort and soothe someone in need, well that was plumb loco. Lettie was the last one to expect it to happen. She barely spoke to anyone, for pity's sake. And she didn't like people in general, so why had she been compelled to do what she did?

She had no explanation of course, which was why she couldn't stop thinking about it. The fact she had also touched him, his bare body no less, weighed on her mind as well. His skin had been cool but smooth and taut as well. Although he had horribly rank body odor, it wasn't repulsive to be close to him. She could still feel him, like the ghost of his form clung to her.

Lettie shook her hand as though to fling away the sensation. She never expected anything good to happen. Life had taught her things were hard until they became harder.

Shane Murphy obviously knew that rule too, judging by the condition of his life.

With a start, she realized she was at the house she lived in, standing at the door like a fool. If she were lucky, no one witnessed her silly woolgathering. Bad enough she was spending time thinking about a stranger, *a man.*

Lettie opened the door quickly and stepped inside. The interior soothed her. Something about the house made her feel safe. It served as both a home and the newspaper office. Due to the generosity of Angeline and her husband, Lettie had been lucky enough to be invited to live there and be responsible for printing the newspaper.

Sometimes when she was with the young married couple, Lettie had to look away, unable to watch her friends be affectionate with each other. It hurt to see what they had, what she would never have, could never have. Angeline seemed to understand because she never made Lettie feel bad for the way she acted.

Angeline was a true friend, someone genuine and pure of heart. Lettie knew she was beyond lucky to live in this house, but she also knew time was ticking away. While she loved Angeline as a sister of her heart, she could not live there forever. They came by the house often—considering Sam owned it and the newspaper, it was expected. Some days Lettie remained at the restaurant late so she didn't have to see them together.

The hourglass was slowly emptying of sand. Someday Lettie would need to move on. It wasn't her house after all. For now, she stayed put, almost content to have a place to call her own, or at least a safe haven to live in.

She walked into the room that held the printing press. This was her place, where she felt at peace. The machine, the ink, the paper, it all made sense to her. Human beings were confusing and unpredictable. This hulking press was a constant companion, whether it was working as intended or not. She could figure it out without involving emotion, except perhaps annoyance. Until arriving in Forestville, she hadn't been around a machine like this one. She'd felt a connection right away, and to her secret delight, Sam had taught her how to use it.

Tonight she didn't need to print the paper, but just being there helped calm her. Strangely enough she found a sparrow feather lying right on top as though someone had left it for her. After brushing it to the floor, she went to work cleaning, intending the activity to take her mind off Shane Murphy. With a rag and some mineral oil, she worked at the ink that had splattered on the sides of the press. She didn't know how much time passed before she sensed she wasn't alone any longer.

"Who was he?" Sam leaned against the doorway. His straight black hair, dark eyes and light copper skin made him stand out as half-Indian. What others saw as something to scorn, Angeline found special.

"Who was who?" Lettie kept at her scrubbing, her fingers now stained with ink.

"Don't be coy, Lettie. That's not your way." His gaze bored into her back. "When a stranger appears in Forestville, it's news."

She sighed and turned to look at him, propping a fist on her right hip. "He's no one. A stranger who was in a bad way. Marta wanted to do him a kindness and doctored him. End of the news."

Oh how she lied. There was so much more to what happened, but she didn't want to share that with Sam, not because he was her friend's husband but because he wrote the news. The last thing she needed was to have folks gossiping about her and the stranger who fell into the Blue Plate, or rather onto her feet.

"The way Dennis Fox tells it, he was dead, and you brought him back to life."

Shock spread through her, turning her mouth dry and making her heart thump hard. "What?"

Sam raised his brows. "A fantastic story, but it's already spread. I heard talk of it at the mercantile."

"Damn." She threw the rag at the machine, unsatisfied with the gentle thwack it made as it hit. "That little booger. I should've gagged him."

"He didn't mean any harm. Besides, it gives people something to talk about besides your growl." Sam's mouth curved into a grin. "Sometimes you do try to be scary, you know."

Lettie didn't want to smile back, but her lips twitched. Sam was one of the few people she would let tease her. It was done out of affection, not out of meanness. He seemed to understand her, perhaps because of Angeline, but she also knew he meant no harm.

She wouldn't expect the same from other folks in town. Dennis's story would spread and only get worse the longer Shane was at the Blue Plate. She had to convince Marta to move the man to the doctor's place as soon as possible.

"He also said you patched him up and let him sleep in your bed."

"It ain't my bed. Hasn't been since I moved in here. That little bastard." Lettie headed for the door. She would find the little shit and holler at him until he stopped spreading tales. Sam blocked her path. His broad shoulders nearly filled the door.

"He's eleven, Lettie. I talked to him, and he changed his mind about telling such stories. I explained how people would think badly of you, and he understood. In fact I think he was remorseful." Sam held up his hands. "You can yell at him if you want, but I think he might be hiding from you already."

Lettie's anger at the boy dissipated in a blink. She didn't want to be the frightening old lady who made children hide from her. That wasn't who she was.

"For what it's worth, I don't think you're scary anymore." He smiled. "Of course you did try to scare me once, but I'm glad you didn't."

Lettie had threatened him with bodily injury if he hurt Angeline, the one person she would kill for. Even then, he understood she was all bluster and no bite. Either that or he knew her anger was her defense and saw behind it. Sam was a good man, the best she'd met in her life. The only person she would trust Angeline with.

"Thank you, I think." She took a deep breath and blew it out, her gut churning. It was probably a good thing she hadn't eaten, or she'd feel worse than she did.

"Why don't you come by for supper tomorrow? Angeline has had her eye on a hen for a few days. Thinking about making chicken and dumplings. All she thinks about is food these days." This time his grin spread from ear to ear. As expectant parents, their happiness grew with each passing moment. Lettie was happy for them, truly she was, but she was too much of a mess on the inside to have children of her own.

Yet another reason to keep away from her friends. It hurt too much to see what they had, knowing she would never have a taste of it in her life. One day she might not be selfish, but for now she did what she had to do.

"I'm working tomorrow night. Alice has some shindig over

in Benson she is going to with a beau, and Karen can't serve the supper crowd alone. We're still short-handed." It was the truth, even if it made it convenient not to visit Angeline and Sam.

His smile fell. "I need to help you find a replacement for Angeline. We'll put an ad in the newspaper next week."

"There isn't anyone in Forestville, so we'll need to throw the papers into the west wind to find someone."

Sam's brows went up. "Did you just make a joke?"

Lettie shook her head. "Now why would I do that? I'm not funny."

He laughed. "I'll have the first drafts ready for you by Monday night." To her surprise, he leaned over and kissed her forehead. "Good night, Lettie."

She stood there for a few minutes after he left, overwhelmed by the strange and crazy day she'd had. Perhaps tomorrow would be more normal, and if she had her way, Shane Murphy wouldn't be part of it for long.

His hands were strong and callused as they ran up and down her legs. The smooth rasp of them on her bare skin raised goose bumps. She arched into his touch, eager for more, wanting to feel his hands all over. He chuckled softly as though he knew what she was thinking.

"More," she ordered.

"Eager, are you?" His voice was like whiskey, smoky and deep. He kissed one knee then the other.

She let her legs fall open, the cool night air bathing her heated core. There was no one who made her feel this way but him. He seemed to know where to put each lick, each kiss, each stroke to maximize her pleasure. There was no book, no conversation, to tell him how to accomplish these feats, only pure instinct. She never wanted another.

His palms skimmed her hips, bypassing her pussy by inches. A small moan crept up her throat as tingles spread through her. Every small hair stood on end. His teasing was almost as pleasurable as the lovemaking. The anticipation made the actual act that much more intense.

When he reached her breasts, he cupped them, circling round the nipples while he kissed his way up her belly. His cock brushed against her knee, then her inner thigh. She held her breath, waiting for more.

His mouth closed around her nipple, and he sucked hard. She thrust her hips up, finding his staff inches away from her aching center. She looked into his smoky eyes.

"My Violet." He entered her in one thrust.

Lettie woke up with her heart pounding and the blood rushing past her ears like a river. She was covered in sweat, her night rail rucked up around her hips, bare to the open air.

It was a dream. A dream.

Her entire body was on fire, burning for the touch of an unknown man in a dream. Oh but he wasn't unknown. Lettie would be lying to herself if she called him that. For sure, it was Shane Murphy. The man's gray eyes were unmistakable.

She swung her legs over the side of the bed and stood up. The night air was sticky and stagnant. She had left the window open in hopes of a breeze, but there wasn't a whisper of one. She poured tepid water into the basin and splashed her face with shaking hands.

Lettie had never found pleasure with a man. Hell, she'd never found pleasure with herself. That part of her was dead or had never worked at all. Or so she'd thought.

Judging by the incredibly erotic dream she just had, that wasn't true at all. What had brought it on? Touching his skin? She hadn't thought anything of it, at least not in that way, when she'd been comforting him. It was the contact of one human being to another, nothing more. It must have awakened something inside her that reared its head while she slept.

To her shame, her nipples were hard and her pussy ached a bit. Her dreams had affected her physically in a way she was at a loss to handle it. Lettie never planned on being with a man again, ever. If she kept dreaming about Shane, something was going to happen, good or bad.

She knew she wouldn't sleep anymore, so she slipped off her damp night rail and hung it on the hook. A rustle in the bushes outside had her in a crouch, her arms crossed around her protectively. It was likely a bird, but it scared her. She crawled over and shut the window as quick as she could, then sat beneath the sash, shaking.

She had to talk to Angeline.

Shane smelled something good, really good. His stomach rumbled then howled as the scent permeated the air around him.

Ham.

He hadn't had good ham in ages, and the memory of curing some in the smokehouse when he was young crowded his mind. Pa had taught him everything he needed to know about being a farmer, and he'd smoked the best ham in the county. Their crops had been healthy, their animals well cared for and life had been good. Of course, war changed everything. The one thing his father couldn't teach was how to be a soldier when there was no more war to fight.

Shane shook off the memories of his father and opened his right eye, the left still stuck shut. The bedside table held a plate of ham, steaming scrambled eggs and biscuits. His stomach scratched at his backbone, begging to be fed.

He glanced around. No one was in the room, but the door was open. The last thing he remembered was talking to Miss Brown, and then nothing.

Wait, he had a sketchy memory of someone calling his name and being afraid. There was an angel, perhaps the granny angel again, saving him. It was a blur, a nightmare dream, hovering at the edge of his mind.

"Good morning, sir." The granny angel stood beside the bed, smiling at him, her words decorated by a German accent. "I make you a plate before the restaurant opens. Are you feeling better?"

"I think so. Had strange dreams." He vaguely remembered one where he'd been making love to a woman, but the details were hazy. She had long legs, which meant it wasn't Vi, who was short as could be. The details of the dream wouldn't come to him, just the feeling, which left him with a hard dick thankfully hidden by the blanket.

If the granny angel tried to check his wounds, she would get an eyeful of something she didn't want to see. He pulled up the blanket a little, embarrassment rushing through him.

She tutted at him. "You must rest today, Mr. Murphy. I will send Lettie up when she gets here. In the meantime, I will feed you."

To his mortification, his stomach growled like a bear rising from hibernation. She grinned and sat on the chair beside the bed.

"You don't have to feed me, ma'am."

"I am Marta, not ma'am." She waved her hand in dismissal. "Until your hands heal, you will need help." She picked up the plate, and he noticed she had already cut the ham into small pieces and mixed it with eggs. A fluffy biscuit topped off the meal.

He couldn't argue with her. The food looked and smelled better than anything he'd had in years. Shane felt odd letting this kind older woman feed him, but the food was as delicious as it smelled. He only ate half before he had to stop. His stomach couldn't hold anymore, although he'd only eaten a child's portion.

"It's okay, *liebchen.* You are healing." She examined his wounds and then smoothed his hair back as though she were his grandmother. "You rest now."

Her gentle touch and acceptance of him made his throat tighten up. Something had brought him to this town, perhaps to heal or to die. Whatever the reason was, he didn't deserve the kindness.

He must have dozed off, likely due to the fact his belly was full to bursting, because when he woke again, Miss Brown was standing over him. Her expression was full of confusion and infinite sadness. He knew that sadness well—he'd lived with it as his daily companion for years.

She started when she noticed his uninjured eye was open. "I didn't know you were awake."

"I was dozing because I ate too much breakfast." He didn't want her to feel self-conscious about staring at him. Although he'd love to know why.

"Marta is an amazing cook. Her eggs are fluffier than any I've ever seen." She gestured to his hands. "Did she feed you, or did you manage on your own?"

"She insisted on feeding me." *Liar.* He could have said no and done it on his own.

"Sounds like Marta." She sat on the chair beside the bed. "I, um, was wondering if you would rather go to the doctor's instead of here. To make you more comfortable."

"If I could walk, I wouldn't be in this bed at all. I appreciate your hospitality, Miss Brown, and I promise I will be gone as soon as I can." These folks had done a great deal for him, and he hadn't done a thing in return. Not that he had anything to give. "When I'm better, I can do some jobs for you to make up for everything."

"I didn't mean to make you feel... Well, never mind. I was thinking because there are lots of women here, you might want to be with the doctor because he's not. A woman that is." She stood and went over to the washstand. "Forget I opened my mouth. I tend to trip over words."

Shane looked away from her awkward fumbling, feeling foolish and useless. "My head feels better this morning."

"Was it hurting bad?" She rung out a rag and turned around with it in her hand.

"Like someone used a hammer on my skull. I could live with the rest of the pains, but that was downright brutal." He hadn't said a thing about any of his discomfort before. He usually kept it to himself. What had possessed him to say it now?

"We could have given you some laudanum for it." She sat back down, her brow furrowed. "Why didn't you say something?"

He tried to shrug but found his shoulders wouldn't work right. "I ain't one to whine about my aches."

Her gaze traveled over his face, and he considered asking for a mirror. No doubt he was unrecognizable, not to mention swollen, bruised and stiff.

"You are stronger than most men then." She reached for the bandage. "I need to clean the wound and put a new bandage on. It's going to hurt."

"I remember you telling me that before."

Her lips twitched, but she didn't smile. "I wanted to warn you, Mr. Murphy."

"Please call me Shane. I ain't been called Mr. Murphy in quite some time." He had been not much of anything in quite some time.

"Marta would say she doesn't think it would be appropriate, but I don't mind. Shane. It's a good Irish name." She started untying the bandage, her face so close to his he noted her eyes were actually several shades of brown, not only one. They were framed by long, thick, dark eyelashes, ones that made a tiny breeze when she blinked.

What a perfectly silly thing for him to notice.

Then he started noticing more, such as the clean scent that surrounded her, and the fact her hair curled around the pink shell of her ears. She wasn't a plain brown bird after all.

"What's your first name?"

Her gaze snapped to his, the bandage hanging from her hand. A few seconds passed and he thought for sure she wasn't going to answer him. "Lettie."

"Thank you for helping me, Lettie."

She turned away and stood. "Without kindness, we lose part of ourselves."

He wondered what she meant by that but didn't necessarily want to know the answer. She took a clean bandage from the washstand and came back to the bed. Her hands trembled slightly.

Was she afraid? Was there some other reason? Shane wanted to know more about her, needed to know. What was it about Lettie that made her different from the other hundreds of people he'd encountered since he left home for good?

She cleaned his wounds with a gentle touch, which was surprising considering his memory of how rough she'd been when he first arrived. Of course the whiskey could have warped that experience. Her hands were strong, the fingers long and elegant. He saw calluses on her hands, yet they weren't ugly at all. They told him this woman worked hard and took pride in what she did.

As she washed his face and neck, she wrinkled her nose. "I think we need to get you into a bath as soon as possible."

"Am I that bad?"

"No, worse than bad." She was definitely blunt. "I'll have Dennis bring up the hip bath and water."

The very idea of taking a bath—he couldn't remember the last time he'd had one—made his gut clench. Would Lettie be bathing him? A hip bath was small, would barely cover his ass much less anything else. He didn't know if he would be strong enough to allow her to bathe him. Logic told him she must have seen most of him already since he only wore his drawers.

"Where are the rest of my clothes?"

She met his gaze again, hers direct and shuttered at the same time. "We burned them. You had, ah, critters in them, and there were more holes than fabric."

Embarrassment waged war with a spurt of anger. "You're saying that if I wanted to leave, I'd have to go in a pair of drawers since I have nothing else to wear. Do you steal from all the people you show kindness to?"

That was the wrong thing to say. Lettie shot to her feet, water spraying on his chest and the sheet.

"I'm going to let that pass by because I know you're suffering. Getting off drink is near impossible without a lot of hurt." She set the rag in the basin. "But if you ever accuse me of stealing again, Mr. Murphy, I won't be showing you any kindness."

With that, she quit the room, basin in hand. Shane's anger disappeared as quickly as it had come. He started shaking again, awake, alert and craving that which he couldn't have. Damn, why did he have to be sober and an ass? Well that was one of the reasons he drank. He was an ass, one who cared only about himself and his needs. One who would let his family be slaughtered while he drank his cares away.

Painful memories pushed at the door he'd erected deep inside his soul. That way lay agony. He could not, would not, let them out. If he did, Shane would put a gun to his head and end the misery before it could overwhelm him.

He managed to push himself into a sitting position, or nearly sitting. The sheet had fallen away, and he realized the drawers he was wearing weren't his. They were a sturdy pair of white cotton, clean and for sure not his. Hanging from hooks on the wall were a brown shirt and trousers. On the floor beneath them sat a pair of used but sturdy boots.

Shame swept through him again. These folks had given him clothes and shoes to wear, doctored his wounds, fed him and kept him alive. What did he do? Accuse them of stealing his flea-bitten clothes. He felt sick at the monumental stupidity of his actions.

The door banged open, and a floppy-haired boy came in. Shane assumed it was Dennis. He was around twelve, gangly as all get out, his hands and feet too large for his skinny frame. As he set the wooden hip bath on the floor, he stared at Shane wide-eyed. A towel lay around his neck, which he carefully put on the very end of the bed, close to the bath but as far from Shane as possible.

"I thought you was dead, mister. I thought Lettie brought you back with her healing touch."

Perhaps she had since Shane was experiencing emotions he had long since buried. Lettie Brown had brought out the human being who had been hiding inside him for six years.

"I don't think it was a miracle, son. She does have a healing touch though." He could see out of his left eye. Only a slit of light, but it was better than it had been. His fingers didn't ache as much either.

Without a word, the boy fled the room, his big feet slapping as he ran down the hall, presumably to get the water for the bath. The knot in his chest loosened a smidge.

The sound of footsteps returning was slower this time, and Dennis appeared in the doorway with two buckets, one in either hand. Steam rose in wisps, winding up around his skinny wrists as he stepped into the room. He set one down then poured the first into the tub, followed quickly by the second.

Again, the boy ran from the room, the thump of his shoes echoing as he made his way downstairs. Shane stared at the tub, at the piping-hot water that awaited him. He leaned down and sniffed at his armpit, and the stench made him gag. How had Lettie been able to doctor him when he smelled like a dead animal left in the sun for three days?

Holy hell, he had let himself scrape along the bottom of life for a long time. Drunk, foolish, starving and stinking. If he hadn't been taken in by the folks at the restaurant, he would likely be dead in a ditch somewhere, forgotten and not missed by anyone.

Was it a kindness? Or a punishment to make sure he suffered more?

Dennis appeared a third time with two more buckets. Presumably cold water was in his left hand since no wisps of steam rose from it. He put the third bucket of hot water in and then looked at Shane. A bar of soap emerged from his pocket, along with a clean rag.

"Miss Marta told me to help you, but I ain't sure what to do."

"I can wash myself if you help me out of bed. It's been a long time since anyone washed me." He managed a lopsided grin. "I don't expect you are keen on doing it either."

Dennis shook his head hard enough to make his floppy hair get in his eyes. "No, sir, I ain't, but Miss Marta says I need to show kindness."

The granny angel had an influence over the folks in the restaurant, a good one too. He had definitely landed in the right place if he wanted to be treated well. Too bad they didn't know who he really was, or they would have left him in the mud outside.

"Then you can show me kindness by helping me stand, then closing the door behind you."

"I can do that." Dennis came around the side of the bed warily.

Shane didn't want to think he scared children, but since he had no idea what he looked like at the moment, he would assume it was because of his injuries. Any other reason would be unacceptable. He wasn't a monster—he was a coward.

The boy was strong, lending his bony frame to Shane's shaky efforts to become upright. By the time he made it to his feet, he was sweating and lightheaded.

"Are you sure you can bathe yourself, mister?"

No he wasn't, but he didn't want to tell Dennis that. "I'll be fine. Just get me over to the tub."

Together they managed to shuffle forward. Dennis led him to the edge of the bed where Shane rested, the towel beneath him. As the boy poured the cold water into the tub, he kept his eye on Shane.

"You don't look so good, mister."

His laugh was nowhere near amused. It was more like a strangled sob. "I'm not so good, Dennis. Thank you for your kindness."

The boy stared at him for a moment longer, then he picked up the bucket from the hot water, leaving one full of cold water, and quit the room.

Shane leaned against the bed, shaking and nauseated, barely able to move an inch closer to the water. He shouldn't have sent the boy away because now the bath would go to waste. With some extra effort, he might be able to scoot backwards onto the bed to save himself the indignity of falling on his face if he attempted to walk.

When the door banged open, he was startled enough to get to his feet. Lettie stood there, anger written in every pore of her body. One look at him and his shaking knees and she closed the door behind her. Quick as lightning she was there, supporting him before he realized he was about to do what he hoped he wouldn't—fall.

"You are an idiot, Shane Murphy."

"You have no idea, Lettie Brown."

"You should have let Dennis help you, foolish man. You can't even, well, for pity's sake, take a piss by yourself."

This time he did laugh. "You sure believe in being honest."

She repeated his words, "You have no idea."

Oh he really did like her. She was certainly not a demure, soft-spoken little thing. Her strength surprised him, considering she was holding up his two-hundred-pound-plus body without effort. She was tall too, her nose nearly even with his chin. Most women were only up to his shoulder in height. Or perhaps the whiskey had made him shrink.

"You are skin and bones, held together by bandages and sheer willpower," she griped as she maneuvered him to the tub. "I hope you don't think I do this every day because I don't." With that, she stripped off his drawers, and he stood in front of her naked as the day he was born.

Shane met her gaze, and a spark of something passed between them. He could hardly believe it, would have trouble accepting it, but damned if his body didn't react to her as a woman. It had been so long since he'd touched a woman, longer since his dick did anything but piss out used whiskey.

Before he could embarrass himself any further, he pulled his gaze from hers and focused on the tub. He used the bed as leverage to lift one foot into the steaming water. It was hot, but not too bad. By the time he had both feet in, she was behind him, steadying his hips with her strong hands. She was inches from his foolish dick, which took the opportunity to twitch and show signs of hardening.

Shit.

He needed to get this bath over with right now before he did something to scare away his brown angel of mercy. Gritting his teeth, he sank as far as he could into the tub, the water barely covering his ass.

"Hand me the soap please." He didn't sound polite even if the words were. Shane needed to get the scrubbing over with.

She dipped the soap in the water by his leg, making his

dick twitch and harden. With a wet slapping sound, she soaped up the washrag vigorously. He had to look away when his imagination decided to think about her rubbing him like that.

He grew another inch and felt another twitch.

What the hell was wrong with him? He shouldn't be attracted to her, to anyone for that matter. He had the touch of death for anyone close to him. Only a heartless monster would allow himself to lose control in this situation. He assumed he was reacting because he was naked and hadn't been with a woman in six years. Logic told him to think about something else.

She started washing his back, her touch firm but not brutal. Shane should protest and tell her to stop, but it felt damn good. More than good. He sighed at the sheer pleasure, his head lolling forward, his eyes closing.

"You have an inch of filth on you, Mr. Murphy."

"Shane," he mumbled.

"Do you think now is a good time to be using your first name?"

He chuckled at her honesty. "Yes I do. You saw me at my worst, Lettie, and now you've seen me at my very worst."

She chuffed a laugh. "I'm helping for purely selfish reasons, Mr. Mur—Shane."

A tiny and decidedly foolish part of him smiled at the selfish part. Was it because she wanted to touch him naked? Of course not.

"You really do stink."

This time he laughed, a rusty sound. "Good thing you're not a delicate flower who would be offended by my manly stench."

"Oh I'm offended all right, which is why I'm making sure

you're clean." She moved to his arms and armpits, and to his surprise, her touch made him laugh. "Are you ticklish?"

"I don't know. I ain't ever been tickled." His life hadn't been silliness and games. Farms needed hard boys and harder men. Shane had been groomed to be a farmer since he could pick up a bucket and milk a cow. The war sent that plan sideways, but war sure as hell didn't involve tickling either.

She paused at his hand, her gaze sliding to his. Without a word, she told him she had never been tickled either. Whatever life she'd led, it had been as hard as his.

"I'll try not to do it anymore." She resumed scrubbing.

He shook his head. "It's okay. I kind of liked it."

She set the washrag on the side of the tub and picked up the bucket of clean water. "I'm going to wet your hair now. I think you need to cut it too."

"Do what you need to. I'm a mess."

The tepid water felt good sluicing down his back, then she started scrubbing at his scalp and he groaned. Years of life and dirt coated him, no more so than in his hair. Tears stung his eyes at the pain and the finality of ridding himself of the filth. He wouldn't call it a baptism, but it surely was a cleansing of his soul, which was black at pitch.

"I'm going to let you clean your bottom half while I go get another bucket of water." She put the washrag on his shoulder. "Soap is on the floor beside you."

He held his breath until the door closed. The sigh that escaped him made ripples in the tiny tub of water. With grim determination he used his bandaged hands to wash his body as best he could, the effort costing him dearly. By the time the door opened again, he shook from head to toe, completely sapped of strength. But he was clean, almost.

"I couldn't get my feet."

"I'll do them after I cut your hair." She set the bucket beside the tub. Her fingers ran through his hair, separating the locks, bringing back the intense memories of her scalp scrubbing. Soon the *snip-snip* was the only sound in the room. He kept his eyes closed, trying desperately to keep his mind blank. However, his stupid dick, which decided to come to life again, kept yanking his thoughts back to Lettie's hands.

He'd never much thought about women's hands before. They did what everyone's hands did. Yet there was something about hers, an indefinable attraction he couldn't ignore. Lettie did not have delicate hands, which was good because she was not a small woman. Her fingers were long but slender and strong. Her palm was wide but not overly so.

The way she'd held him steady as he stepped into the bath, the way she washed his skin and especially the way she scrubbed his scalp sent a shiver down his body that had nothing to do with the temperature of the water or the room. Damned dick hardened even more.

"That ought to give you some relief." She put the scissors down with a small clink on the wood floor. "I've got to rinse."

He made a strangled sound, willing away the blood rushing through him as she touched him once more. The water, her fingers and the aroused state of his body all conspired together.

"There, it'll do for a haircut in a tub." The bucket made a clang as she set it back down. "Stand up so I can wash your feet real quick."

Oh hell. He probably did not have the strength to stand without help, and his erection was currently waving at him in greeting. Two reasons why he could not possibly stand.

"I think I need to sit here for a spell." His voice sounded weak.

"We also need to change the bandages on your hands. I'm not going to wait around with a naked man in a tub. Get up, Shane." She put her arms beneath his and pulled him to his feet. The water splashed on the floor and, he was sure, on her since she hovered behind him.

His cock, on the other hand, stood at attention like a good soldier. He gritted his teeth, waiting for her reaction.

"Put your hand on my shoulder and lift up your left le—" She stopped in mid-sentence, her gaze glued to his staff. Her face flushed a soft shade of pink.

A beat, then two, passed. She stared, he grew harder, the air grew thicker. Shane didn't know whether to laugh or cry at the situation. Whatever he did, something needed to happen.

He put his hand on her shoulder and lifted his leg so she could wash his foot.

"I...uh... That is... Shit on a shingle. Why not." To his surprise, Lettie washed his foot, then waited while he switched legs. She didn't mention the dick nearly staring her in the face. The woman had grit, that was for damn sure.

"I'm sorry." His apology was heartfelt if not as well said as it could have been.

"It ain't the first time I've seen a man's parts before. I was married once. He's dead now." Her voice was flat, devoid of any emotion. What kind of idiot jackass had she been married to? This was a woman any man would be proud to call his own. She was hard-working, handsome, smart and strong.

"Me too. Married once, I mean." Shane could hardly believe he'd confessed that to her, to anyone. "She died."

Oh how those two words summed up an ocean of pain and sorrow, of guilt and shame. How could there be a way to explain what happened? There couldn't and there wouldn't. That was as far as he would go to tell anyone the truth. The rest of it would fester inside him until he died, eaten alive by what he'd done.

Her gaze flew to his, and she seemed to search his face for something. "My condolences on losing your wife." She meant what she said. Her honesty never skipped a beat.

"Thank you. It's been almost seven years." Why did he keep talking? Lettie was someone who brought out what he'd been keeping inside, whether or not he liked it. He had no idea what that meant either.

"Maybe it's time to move on." Lettie walked behind him and placed a towel on his shoulders. "Now step out of the tub. Don't worry, I've got you."

Her first comment cut like a knife, stealing his breath for a moment. She didn't know him, had no idea why he hadn't moved on. Lettie was like a confessor, not offering absolution but hard advice instead. He wanted to scream at her, tell her it was none of her business and that he couldn't move on. Yet he didn't. He had been the one who opened his mouth and told her about Vi, so why should she bear his wrath? Lettie had been blissfully ignorant of his widower status until he opened his mouth.

Her amazing hands held his hips as he stepped from the tub. Emotions ricocheted through him, dark and raw. He couldn't control or identify them. As soon as he got his balance, he spun around until he faced her.

The moment stretched out, his heart's *thump-thump* echoing through him. As he stared down at her brown eyes, she blinked, her expression a mixture of confusion and need.

Slowly, ever so slowly, he shifted closer until he was an inch from her. Time stopped around them. He lowered his head until their lips met, the briefest touch, then once more, harder and more insistent. Her lips were soft but firm, moving slightly under his for a fraction of a second. She stepped back, her shaking fingers pressed against her mouth.

"I need to get fresh bandages." She almost ran from the room. The door rattled in the frame as she closed it with force but not quite slamming it.

He stood there, breathing hard, dick pulsing, heart galloping. Shane wanted to do more than sneak a couple kisses. He needed to feel her from head to toe, to taste her skin, her breasts, her pussy. He wanted to fuck her until both of them found release.

Shane wanted Lettie.

The truth crashed into him as though he'd been kicked. It stole his breath. For the first time in his life, Shane wanted someone other than his late wife in his arms. Agony ripped through him full force, and he staggered to the bed. He'd forgotten what real pain felt like, one not dulled by whiskey. He had nothing to offer her, a stranger who had brought him back from the dead.

There was no future for the two of them. She knew it. He knew it. Now if he could only forget the last fifteen minutes and slide back into the hole he had existed in two days ago. Of course that wasn't going to happen. Fate had brought him here for a reason. He sure as hell hoped it wasn't to die of a broken heart again.

Chapter Three

Lettie ran out of the restaurant, leaving a startled group staring after her. She knew the front of her was wet, and no doubt she looked like she'd seen a ghost. Truth was, she was scared senseless over what had happened, *no*, by how she'd felt when it happened.

She liked kissing Shane. So much so that she wanted to do more.

Lettie needed to understand what that meant. She had never enjoyed kissing or doing a man's business with him. Hell, she would have been happy never to touch a man again.

Then Shane Murphy fell into her life.

His lips were soft and warm, perfect against hers. The moment had been pure magic. Every second of it was burned into her memory—the smell of his freshly scrubbed skin, the way his shorn hair felt beneath her fingers, the sight of his naked body, and most of all, the tingles that raced through her when he kissed her.

She had no idea what to do. It wasn't supposed to be like that. She didn't need a man, much less one who was a worse mess than she was. Yet here she was, tied in a knot and running. She needed to talk to Angeline now for sure. The dream, the bath, the kiss, the naked man. It was too much to sort out.

Her rapid pace got her to Angeline's door in ten minutes, normally a fifteen-minute walk. By the time she knocked on the door, she was breathing harder than she should have, and her heart beat so fast it hurt. Even her knock was a staccato rhythm, sharp and fierce.

It seemed like an hour before Angeline opened the door. She started to smile until she saw Lettie's face. "What happened?"

"I don't know. I...um... Well...that is, he kissed me."

Angeline's blue eyes widened. "Oh my." She took hold of Lettie's arm. "Get in here."

Lettie stumbled inside, Angeline closing the door behind her. They walked into the kitchen to find Sam at the table with a cup of coffee and a book. He watched them both as they approached, his expression guarded.

"Lettie came by." Angeline didn't ask her husband to leave or explain why Lettie was there.

Without saying a word, he picked up and quit the room, cup and book in hand. Another shining example of how connected the two of them were. They spoke to each other with just a glance. Lettie would have to be staked out beside an anthill and covered with honey before she would admit it, but she wanted what they had. Enough that she ached at night, alone, and aware she would be that way for the rest of her life.

Angeline led her to the table and pointed at the chair her husband had vacated. "Sit."

While her friend fussed in the kitchen with the pot of coffee, Lettie sat down. She let out a breath slowly, her stomach flipping every which way. She didn't know how to tell Angeline everything. Some of it was downright embarrassing and too personal. Yet she had to do something or spend her days hiding from Shane, or worse, leave Forestville altogether.

Angeline set two steaming mugs on the pristine tabletop—a gift from Sam's wealthy aunts. She took Lettie's hand and squeezed it.

Lettie took a sip of the hot brew, grateful for the bitter burn as it slid down her throat. Although she certainly wasn't cold in the summer air, the coffee seemed to chase away a chill that had taken hold of her. She didn't know how to start telling her friend about everything that had happened.

"Coffee's good." An inane thing to say, but at least it was words.

"Sam is very good at making coffee. He said he learned in the Army because he didn't want to drink the sludge the other soldiers made." Angeline chuckled, perhaps to break the tension.

Lettie took another gulp of the steaming brew. "I had a dream last night." She paused, her mind full of images from the very erotic meanderings of her subconscious.

Angeline waited patiently, sipping at her coffee.

"It, uh, well, it was about the stranger, Shane."

Her friend's brow furrowed. "You're using his first name?"

Lettie waved her hand. "Let me tell this before I lose the nerve."

"I'm sorry. Please keep going. I promise I'll stay quiet." Angeline sat back, her expression open and listening.

"It was the first time I had a dream like this. I've never, um, well you know that I never found pleasure in my marriage, with a man." Lettie waited while Angeline acknowledged that with a small nod. "I didn't think I could, like maybe that part of me was busted or didn't work right. Then I had this dream."

Angeline appeared to be completely absorbed in what Lettie was telling her. The coffee sat on the table, forgotten. "And this stranger, Shane, was in the dream?" she prompted.

Lettie closed her eyes and conjured up the image of him kissing her splayed legs. She shivered at the memory. "He pleasured me, in the dream that is. And more. I ain't gonna say details 'cause that's going to make it harder to tell."

While she masked it quickly, Angeline's expression told Lettie she was disappointed to miss the details. Lettie wasn't worried about that—her friend had a very happy marriage with a man who likely pleasured her daily.

"When I woke up I was still feeling the dream, if you know what I mean. I was out of sorts and decided to ask Marta to move the man to the doc's place." Lettie paused to take another gulp of coffee, annoyed to see her hands shaking again. "She wouldn't hear of it, of course. I got mad and marched up there to make him move. He was sleeping peaceful-like, and before I could tell him to get out, he opened his eyes."

Lettie set the cup on the table. "The memory from the dream was hanging on me like a coat, weighing me down. I couldn't look at him without remembering what the dream Shane did to me, with me."

Angeline squeezed her hands. "I'm sorry, honey."

"I made this crazy decision and had Dennis bring up bath water for Shane."

Angeline whistled. "The hip tub?"

"Yes, the hip tub." Lettie hung her head. "I had to see if what I imagined was real or not."

There was another pause. "You are killing me with waiting, Lettie. You'd best tell me or I might expire on the spot."

Lettie could barely get a breath past the tightness in her throat. "When I saw him, I-I felt the same things all over again, from the dream. He was dirty as a pig in a wallow. But at the same time, he looked like he had in my imaginings."

He was more than that though. Shane was perfectly made, a bit skinny, but just right in so many ways. Lettie had never given anyone else a bath before, and she had let instinct guide her. His skin had been taut and smooth beneath her hands, and very warm. She never expected to enjoy touching another human being, much less a man. Yet the longer she washed him, the greater her need grew to keep touching him.

"I must have made him feel good because when he stood up, well, his part was hard." Lettie felt her cheeks heat. It was completely unlike her to let her emotions get all tangled up enough to blush.

"He enjoyed your touch."

"I reckon so." Lettie glanced down at her hands. "I ain't delicate, that's for sure."

"What else happened?" Angeline peered at her.

"He kissed me," she blurted, then shot to her feet, unable to look her friend in the face. Before marrying Josiah, she had never kissed a boy. No one in their ward had been attractive to her, and she didn't have any boys knocking on the door to court her.

The marriage bed had taught her nothing but discomfort and pain, humiliation and shame. She had no idea how to behave around a man who didn't want to force her or use her. Shane evoked feelings that were confusing.

"Did you kiss him back?" Angeline's quiet question felt more like a pinch, startling and unexpected.

Lettie gripped the windowsill and looked out at the lake beyond. It had been the idyllic spot to build a house, the place both Angeline and Sam loved. The sun's reflection on the water was bright enough to make her eyes sting. She watched a heron glide down and land by the edge of the lake, then poke its beak into the water for some dinner. The entire scene promised peace, if only such a thing existed in her world.

"Did you kiss him back?" Angeline repeated.

Lettie pressed her forehead against the cool glass. "Yes." It was barely a whisper of sound, a tiny acknowledgment of her sin.

"It's okay to be attracted to a man, Lettie. It's normal."

Lettie swung around with a snarl in her heart. "I ain't normal and it ain't okay. I don't want these feelings muddling around inside me anymore. Shane almost ruined everything."

Anger was good. Anger helped her overcome the feelings of panic and discomfort running rampant through her.

Angeline frowned. "You *are* normal and it *is* okay. You're a beautiful, intelligent woman who shouldn't live her life in the shadows of a nightmare she had to live." Tears filled her eyes. "I love you like a sister, Lettie. I can't stand to see you put yourself down so much that you can't have a beau."

"I don't want a beau." Her voice was thin again, dammit.

"Life doesn't ask permission. It happens."

"It needs to unhappen then." Lettie crossed her arms and widened her stance. "I don't want any more dreams, and I sure as hell don't want to be kissing Shane Murphy."

Angeline continued to frown, her expression almost one of pity. Lettie put up with a lot, but pity wasn't one of them.

"I thought coming over here would help, but I don't need you to feel sorry for me." She turned to leave, ignoring her friend's protests. It didn't matter what anyone said, Lettie knew better. She wasn't meant to be with anyone except herself. Life had happened already, and there wasn't much else to be said about it. At least talking to Angeline had fired her up, given her something to hang on to besides confusion.

What she needed to do was ignore Shane Murphy until he was gone, run herself into the ground until she was so exhausted she couldn't dream, and then life would unhappen.

She could go back to being who and what she was. No more confusion and no more kissing.

Her mind made up, Lettie returned to the Blue Plate. It was nearly dinnertime and she had to get to work.

Angeline contemplated going after Lettie, try to get her to see reason. Yet she knew it was futile. Her friend was like a mule, stubborn and unmovable. Talking wasn't her way at all, and her surprise visit proved things were definitely off kilter.

Lettie had shunned all men since they left Utah more than a year ago. She was almost always angry, using her temper to keep the rest of the world away. Inside she had been damaged, physically and emotionally, by their husband Josiah Brown. He was an aberration against all men, not just men of the Latter-day Saints. Angeline harbored no ill will against the people she'd left behind. They had their beliefs and their ways.

She had a new life, a new husband and a baby on the way. Things were about as perfect as they could be for her. It was Lettie's turn to find that same happiness. It appeared to Angeline as though Shane Murphy was the right man for Lettie. Her friend had never taken to any man, much less kissed one.

Angeline needed to help Lettie see what a gift she'd been given. When life offered such a precious opportunity, you had to snatch it with both hands. Lettie had her hands behind her back, so it was up to Angeline to get her to open her arms and take what was in front of her.

Sam poked his adorable face around the corner. "What was that all about? I thought she might rip the door off the hinges."

Angeline smiled. "I think she's falling in love."

Sam's brows went nearly to his hairline. "You don't say?

Now that is a miracle."

"Oh you!" Angeline threw a biscuit at him. He caught it in midair with a grin. "You are going to help me."

He paused. "I am? What am I doing? You know I've got those chairs to finish for—"

"Oh no you don't. You are definitely going to help me find a way to get Lettie and Shane together."

Sam made a face like a five-year-old told to eat his spinach. "Aw, Angel, why me?"

"Because I need help, and you're my partner in everything, right?"

"Dirty tactics, Mrs. Carver." He sauntered over, his lean-hipped swagger and devilish grin sending a shiver up her spine. "If I'm to help, I might need motivation."

She giggled and waited for him. "I think I can do that."

He pulled her against him, and she wrapped her arms around his neck. After being married less than a year, she still shivered when he came near, melted when his calloused hands touched her skin. She wanted Lettie to find that perfect mate. It was what her friend deserved.

"What's your plan, general?" he asked as he nibbled Angeline's ear.

"We're going to play matchmaker."

Sam groaned and buried his face in her neck. Angeline laughed and hugged her husband tight. If she had any say in the matter, Lettie would be doing the same thing very soon.

Shane told himself he wasn't disappointed when a different brown-haired woman brought him dinner. She was nice enough and said her name was Karen. She chatted about her son

Dennis, the floppy-haired boy who had taken care of the tub and water for him. The company was welcome, if not the woman he wanted to see.

Lettie seemed to have disappeared entirely.

With each meal that passed, he hoped to see Lettie, but someone else always brought him his food. There was a young pretty thing named Alice who gave him the evil eye as though he'd already harmed her, Karen, the granny angel and an older man named Pieter who sported blond hair liberally sprinkled with gray. Everyone who worked at the restaurant brought him meals, except Miss Lettie Brown.

Shane hadn't allowed himself to feel emotions for so long that finding someone who evoked a response from him was a pure miracle. His heart and soul had been blackened, burned in the fire of his shame and guilt. With Lettie, he'd transformed into a phoenix, rising from the ashes, whether he wanted to or not. Her straightforward ways, brassy and outspoken, called to whatever was left of him deep inside.

She had no idea what kind of sleeping monster she'd awakened. His belly was full, his wounds healing, and the doctor had been impressed by Lettie's doctoring. Hell, Shane had a clean bed for free, strangers fed him, emptied the chamber pot and made sure his bandages were changed. What more could he ask for?

Lettie.

Three long days went by without seeing her. By then, Shane was itchy, grumpy and annoyed. By his count, it was Friday and he'd been at the restaurant nearly a week. He hadn't felt physically good in at least ten years, since before the war when life had been perfect and his soul unstained.

When the door opened, he turned to look, expecting Alice, who had been bringing breakfast each day, but it was Lettie.

She held a plate of breakfast and a mug of coffee. Her expression was blank, but her jaw twitched as though she was clenching it.

"Where have you been?" he blurted.

She scowled. "I do have to work, Mr. Murphy. Not all of us get by on the kindness of strangers."

Oh that one hurt. He winced inwardly. "I'm thankful for everything you folks have done for me. I would appreciate it if you didn't throw your kindness in my face."

"I didn't mean... That is, I don't always say things right." She seemed flustered, and her cheeks flushed a light pink. It made some freckles on her nose appear, ones he hadn't noticed were there.

As she set the plate down on the table beside the bed, he reached for her, and she flinched. Shane's stomach dropped to his feet. He had thought their kisses had been mutual. They sure as hell felt that way, especially by the second one. Now he realized she was afraid of him. That wasn't what he wanted. The very idea made him sick.

"I'm sorry for what I done, Lettie. I didn't mean to scare you."

"You didn't scare me," she scoffed, but he saw a flash of something behind her eyes, a hint of what she truly felt. She had been scared.

"I haven't kissed anyone in seven years." He hadn't meant to share that piece of information. With anyone. Ever. What kind of idiot was he becoming?

Cocking her head, she finally looked at him, really looked at him. "I think you're being honest."

"I am. I don't know what happened, but I like your company, Lettie." That was safe enough, he hoped.

"That makes one person who does." She put her hands on her hips. "Do you need help sitting up?"

"I don't understand. Do you mean people don't like you?" Shane recognized she was rough around the edges, but she was a good person. Surely people could see that, beneath the gruff ways she showed the world.

"I ain't here to talk about my social status in town. The food's getting cold, so you might want to eat it before it does." She pointed at the pillow. "Do you need help sitting up?"

He pushed himself into a sitting position, pleased to see a bit of surprise on her face. "Nope."

She glanced at his bandaged hands. "I suppose I need to feed you then." The possibility did not sound like fun apparently.

"I can do it." He would do it himself even if he rebroke his fingers to feed himself. Damn woman. She made him act like a foolish man.

Lettie handed him the plate and fork, leaving the coffee on the table. She crossed her arms and waited by the bed, towering over him. It was more like having a schoolmarm beside him than someone he considered a friend, or close to it anyway.

"Are you going to watch me eat?" He managed to pick up a forkful of eggs and take a bite. His annoyance fled when he tasted the salty goodness on his tongue.

She shrugged. "Marta yelled at me enough today. I don't want to go back to the kitchen too soon."

He truly wanted to tell her to leave, but he was glad enough to have her company again, even if she didn't want to be there. Shane ate the rest of the eggs and ham awkwardly, but he got it in his mouth, for the most part. Lettie sighed whenever food landed on his chest, as though he were a child to be chastised for making a mess.

67

"You could have brought a napkin or towel." He frowned up at her.

"You could have eaten slower instead of shoveling it in like you haven't eaten in a month." Her sharp tone made him pause, the piece of bread halfway to his mouth. She must have seen something in his gaze because she closed her eyes and leaned her chin down toward her chest. "I don't try to be mean, I swear I don't."

Shane didn't know how to respond to that so he didn't. When he took a bite of the bread, which was heavier than he'd expected, he paused in mid-chew. It was awful, the worst food he'd had the entire time he'd been at the restaurant.

"It's bad isn't it?" Her tone was unsure, hesitant, a first for her, at least around him.

"Um, yeah, it's bad. Hell I could make better bread than this." He set it back on the plate. "Is there a slop bucket this can be hidden in?"

She flinched. "Are you saying it's fit for pigs?"

"Maybe, if they're not too picky." He had broken his leg as a child, spent six months recovering at home with his mother. She'd taught him how to bake to keep him from nagging her to pieces. Shane wasn't joking when he said he could make better bread—he was an excellent bread maker. It was something he didn't share with most folks since men weren't supposed to be skilled at women's work.

She pinched her lips together and grabbed the plate, heading for the door. Lettie was leaving him alone. Again.

Not if he could help it.

Lettie was quaking in her shoes, scared to do anything but run. She was definitely not the fighter like Angeline. Nope,

Lettie ran from battles, like a yellow coward afraid of her own shadow. Her stomach quivered as she turned the knob.

"Why do you hate me so much?"

Taken aback by the question, she turned to look at him. His face, which she could now see clearly without the swelling, was handsome as sin even with a rainbow of healing bruises. More handsome than she'd expected. His expression and his question reflected confusion and, to her surprise, hurt.

"I don't hate you." Her voice came out in a whisper. "I hate myself."

The shock of the statement rippled through her, making her heart flip once, then twice. She hadn't meant to say that, certainly didn't mean it. Did she?

He tried to climb out of the bed but fumbled with the bedclothes since his hands were still bandaged. She turned back to the door to flee. Lettie had to get out of the room or she might explode. Panic clawed at her when Shane's arm landed on her shoulder. She reached back and hit until he dropped his hand. The hiss of pain told her she had hurt him, but she couldn't worry about that now.

"Lettie, please."

"Let me go." Her voice came out as a sob, one full of desperation.

"No." He pulled her into his arms, but she resisted. Surprised to find he was at least half a head taller than her, a hysterical laugh flew from her mouth. He was so tall, so *big*. How had she bathed him without noticing? As she fought against his grip, he held on firmly but without squeezing her.

"Please." The word she swore she would never use with a man again. Yet she'd said it, desperate to escape, shaking with fear.

"I can't." He tucked her head into the crook of his neck, the scent of man, of Shane, filling her nose. It was a familiar, comfortable scent, but his touch was not.

She needed to get away from him, to find the peace she'd lost a week prior when he fell into her life. Perhaps if she stayed away from him this time, as she had been unable to do, life would be normal once more. Although normal for Lettie was not what others had. Her dark existence wasn't really a life, it simply was.

"I don't know what brought me here, Lettie. Maybe something thought we might need each other." His voice was thick with some unnamed emotion. "I got nothing but this."

"I'm scared." She wasn't scared of his touch, or of him—she was scared of how she felt around him, and how he made her feel. His arms wrapped around her as though God had made them the perfect length to hold Lettie. Stupid thoughts from a stupid woman.

He held her, both of them shaking from emotion or exhaustion—probably a combination of both. She couldn't, or wouldn't, pull away, not yet. Lettie didn't want to lose the experience of being held. It was the first time in her life anyone had touched her so tenderly. She'd never been hugged, except by Angeline. Being in Shane's embrace was an exquisite moment of pureness she'd not known existed.

She didn't realize she was crying until his shirt, the one borrowed from Pieter, grew wet beneath her cheek. Still she held back, unwilling to lose herself in a man again. Even Shane. Tears were supposed to be over for good.

This time when he kissed her, she didn't run. She learned what it meant to kiss someone. His lips were soft as flower petals, moving gently over hers, back and forth across her mouth. He kissed her full on the mouth, then her cheeks, her eyelids, her forehead, and finally the top of her head. It wasn't sexual at all, it was affection, or at least she assumed that was what it was. The entire experience was like a dream, one she hadn't yet had until now.

"Lettie." His voice was ragged, full of the same ancient pain that pervaded her soul. His breath was hot on her hair, his heart thumping steadily against hers. His scent was intense, filling her. He was so alive, so much so she became overwhelmed by him, by this.

This little bit of what she could never have was over. It had to be, because Lettie was too damaged inside and out for anything else. She managed to find her voice. "I can't be who you need."

His chuckle was rusty. "I don't know what I need, honey, but I'm sure I can't be who you need either."

Honey.

It was a simple word, one she heard all the time from one person to another. No one in her life had ever called her honey, or darling, or sweetheart, or anything other than her name, or something worse. In his voice, she heard affection, the one thing that could be so dangerous to both of them.

Up close, she saw his eyes were not simply the color of ashes. They were a swirling mix of grays, full of an aching loneliness she recognized too well.

He kissed her once more, so lightly she almost didn't feel it. "You make me want to be a man again."

Lettie didn't want that responsibility, and she wasn't woman enough for any man, that was for sure. Yet his words touched her heart, like he'd reached in and plucked a string that vibrated through her. She made him want to be better. She did that. Lettie Brown, a woman who didn't know the first thing about being female.

"You are a foolish man." She couldn't help but be honest, seeing as how they were touching chest to thighs, closer than ticks on a dog's ass.

"You won't meet another man more foolish than me." He cupped her face, his thumbs wiping away traces of tears. "Don't cry, Lettie."

The reminder was like a bucket of cold water. She pulled back and wiped her eyes as though she could rub away the emotion that accompanied them. "Ain't nothing can happen, Shane. Ever."

"I know." His sigh came from somewhere near his toes, deep and long. "I was planning on packing up my things tomorrow and heading out."

"What things?" She managed to get a few inches between them. The air felt cooler, and she could breathe again. Think again. "Your clothes were worse than rags, and your boots had more holes than sole."

He glanced down at the shirt and drawers. "These are Pieter's."

"Yep, they are."

"I can't take them."

"You can't walk around town buck naked either. Although it would get you a bed in the jail for a spell." She was starting to babble, pushing away the thought of Shane leaving for good. It had to happen, it had to, but she didn't have to like it. There was no doubt in her mind that her dreams would be filled with memories of the last five minutes. She would have to find a way to forget how she felt and forget him.

He smiled, and she caught her breath at the way it made his eyes crinkle and his handsome face devastating. Shane Murphy was a brown-haired distraction who had to leave Forestville. She couldn't stand seeing him, knowing how good he smelled, felt and kissed. No sirree, she would leave town if he didn't. Either that or go completely loco.

"That might be worth it if you came to visit me." He reached for her again, and she backed up until she hit the door. His smile faded, replaced by that sad expression once more.

One of them had to remember what a terrible idea it was to steal more than a kiss or two. Therein lay additional pain and heartache. Neither one of them was prepared for that.

"I can't. You can't stay." She found the knob with the hand behind her back. "I'll make sure you have supplies to take with you."

As Lettie turned to leave, he sighed again, this time one so fierce, it hit her full force. It was one of sorrow, of loneliness, of an ache so deep it would never be filled. It echoed through her, making her throat tight and her damn eyes sting.

"I'll miss you, Lettie." His words were soft enough she barely heard them.

And her heart wept silent tears for what she could never have.

Angeline came in through the back door of the restaurant. Marta was bent over the stove, peering into a stew as though she could see the future in its bubbling depths. She glanced up, and surprise lit her face.

"Ah, *liebchen*, so good to see you." She set the wooden spoon down and pulled Angeline into her arms.

They hugged for a moment then separated. Angeline had found the mother she'd never known in the German woman and the father she loved more than her own in her husband Pieter. They had been amazingly generous, loving and kind to her and

Lettie. She treasured the older couple as gifts she'd never expected to receive.

When she'd arrived in Forestville with Lettie a year earlier, Angeline had been scared and running from a husband who was more monster than man. The Gundersons had been more than generous, providing a job, a place to sleep and a place to belong. The Blue Plate had become a haven, safe and comfortable. A home.

"It's good to see you too." Her smile was so wide it made her cheeks hurt.

Marta gestured to her belly. "The baby is good? You are good?"

"Yes, we're both fine. I didn't have much morning sickness, and I'm starting to have much more energy." She took Marta's floury hand. "I didn't come by to talk about me though. I want to talk to you about Lettie. And Mr. Murphy."

Marta's brows went up. "You are seeing what I see then, ya? There is something, but both are too stubborn to see it."

"Yes, I see it in Lettie even though I've never met him." She sat at the table with Marta. "Lettie is afraid, scared to take a chance on anything that might hurt her. I want to help her find the happiness she deserves."

"Yes, yes, this is good." Marta nodded, her blue eyes bright. "What do we do?"

"We need to keep Mr. Murphy here in Forestville as long as possible. He came in on the freight wagon, from what I hear, but I don't think he has a job." Angeline lowered her voice. "We need to find him one."

Marta clapped her hands together. "This is marvelous! I think I have the perfect job for Mr. Murphy."

Angeline leaned forward and conspired with Marta.

Together they would help their friend and the man she could love.

The room was filled with a warm glow from half a dozen candles on a table in the corner and on the chest of drawers. She wore a diaphanous nightdress, far fancier than anything she'd ever seen, much less touched or worn. It felt deliciously naughty against her skin. Her nipples peaked as soon as the fabric slid on.

She eagerly waited for him to arrive, the room prepared for seduction. The small knock at the door had her pulse thumping. She turned the knob with damp palms. When she saw his beloved face, her nervousness blew away like a puff on the wind.

He stepped in and closed the door behind him, the key making a gentle snick in the lock. His gray eyes widened when he noticed what she wore. A little whistle escaped from him.

"You look beautiful."

Her cheeks warmed at the compliment. She knew she wasn't really beautiful. However to know he thought she was, well, that made her heart flutter like a trapped butterfly.

"Thank you."

He reached for her hands and opened her arms, pushing her breasts up against the soft fabric. The material was nearly see-through, letting him peek at her gorgeous form. As his gaze started on a second journey from her head to her feet, she made an impatient noise in her throat.

"Kiss me."

He let her hands go and saluted her. With a grin, he snatched her close, his mouth connecting with hers in a clash of lips and tongue. In moments, she was on fire for him, only him. She could hardly catch her breath so great were the waves of arousal that washed over her.

His lips left hers and made their way to her neck. The trail of heat sent goose bumps across her skin, making her nipples ache and her pussy throb. She couldn't wait to feel his mouth in other places on her body. He sucked at her earlobe then blew on the wet skin.

"Mmm, that feels good."

"I'm just getting started, honey."

His hands traveled down her back until he reached her ass. He kneaded her round behind, pulling her close until her softness met his already hard cock. She fairly vibrated with need, feeling his arousal mixing with hers, the heat building rapidly.

"You're wearing too many clothes."

He chuckled. "I'm trying not to rip this flimsy thing off you. God, how you make me crazy, woman." He thrust against her belly, and she closed her eyes, reveling in the rush of tingles spreading through her from the contact.

"Do that again."

He complied, much to her delight. His hands tugged at the pretty nightdress, pulling it up until she had to raise her arms. The beautiful garment fluttered to the ground, leaving her naked.

The feel of the rough fabric of his clothes was more sensual than touching his bare skin. Her nipples hardened, scraping deliciously against his shirt, her pussy becoming wetter with each pass.

"Sorry, darlin', but I gotta taste those tits." He dropped to his knees and took one breast into his mouth. The hot, wet recesses welcomed her aching nipples. He sucked at her while his hand settled on the other side, tweaking and pinching.

Her knees trembled with each tug of his mouth. A throb grew fiercer in her lower belly, and she wanted more. She pulled at his hair and spread her legs.

"Touch me."

Without any more instruction, his free hand landed between her legs. "Oh God, you're so wet."

"Mmm, enough talking, time for doing."

He rubbed her clit with his thumb while two fingers traveled up inside her, fucking her slowly. The combined sensation of his mouth and his hand made her knees weak. She moaned low and deep in her throat. He left one breast for the other, biting the nipple.

She sucked in a breath and hoped he did it again. The feel of his teeth on her over-sensitized nipple was better than expected. He kissed, nibbled and licked at her while his talented hand rubbed her nubbin of pleasure faster and faster.

The orgasm built within her, spreading out from her belly to her pussy and her tits. She threw her head back and called his name as she came. The waves of ecstasy crashed over her, pulling her down until she found herself on her back on the bed. He let her breast go with a mischievous smile, then licked her pussy once.

"Like honey, sweet and tangy. I'm gonna have to taste that later." He shucked his clothes so fast she barely saw him move.

She floated on air, but the pulsing need in her body grew again as his nude form was revealed. He was perfect, muscular, with dark hair on his chest swirling around the flat nipples. Her tongue itched to lick him as he had licked her, then perhaps bite the tiny buds. His cock stood at attention, straight and tall in the nest of dark hair. She clenched in anticipation of having that rod deep inside her.

He lay down on top of her, his heat surrounding her, his skin gently brushing against hers. The contrast between his male power and her feminine softness was made stronger when they were touching from head to toe.

Her body nearly sighed in pleasure from stroking him, feeling the rasp of his whiskers against her cheek, the tickle of his chest hairs against her nipples. It was a myriad of sensations, each one sending a zing through her like ripples in a pond.

His staff nudged her entrance as his knees moved hers farther apart. She closed her eyes, eager to join with him. Her belly quivered in anticipation, waiting, waiting, waiting for him to do more than tease her.

Yet he didn't move any farther. Instead he started kissing her neck and gently rocking in and out, an inch, no more. She pulled at his shoulders, but he didn't increase his cadence or stop kissing her.

"Put it in."

"Bossy woman." He moved to the other side of her neck, her aching nipples rubbing against his chest. She sucked in a breath, momentarily distracted by his technique.

Then she realized he'd completely removed his cock from her pussy, and it hovered there without entering her.

"If you don't put it inside me right now, I may have to punch you." She bit his shoulder, and he laughed. He *laughed*. "Are you making fun of me?"

"No, honey, I'm not." He looked at her with a smile, his gray eyes full of sweet emotion. "I love you, and you have no idea how hard it is not to plunge into you."

"Oh I know how hard it is. I can feel it on my thigh." She

pulled at his ass. "No more teasing."

His expression sobered, and he leaned down, his lips almost but not quite touching hers. His breath was a puff of heat against her skin. "As you wish, my lady."

His mouth came down on hers as he thrust into her pussy. She gasped at the sensation, pleasure ricocheting through her. His tongue invaded her mouth as his dick plundered her core. The simultaneous sensation was indescribable. She could hardly catch a mouthful of air or a thought.

Then he began to move, a quick thrust in, followed by a slow slide out. Again, and again. She squirmed against him, needing more speed, more something. She didn't know what, but the spiraling urge inside her couldn't be ignored.

She scratched at his back, and he seemed to understand. His tempo increased as did her pleasure. Faster. Harder. More. More. More.

Close, so very close. Her pussy began to contract, tighter and tighter, like a spring that was being wound by a master clockmaker. She pulled her mouth away from his as her orgasm hit with the force of a twister.

Round and round, tugging her this way and that, the intensity rocked her to her very soul. She may have shouted or possibly whispered his name in her pleasure. It was him she thought of, loved, needed. He thrust in deep, deeper than she thought possible, and spilled his seed inside her.

Each of them was lost in the whirling climax of the most powerful joining they'd ever known. Tears stung her eyes, and she tried to blink them away before he noticed. When he finally lifted his head and smiled, she felt the stinging once more.

"I love you, Lettie."

Lettie woke up shouting, her body on fire, her night rail twisted around her hips, pulse pounding like a drum hard enough to make her ears hurt. She sucked in a shaky breath and tried to figure out exactly what had happened. With fumbling hands, she managed to turn up the wick on the lantern sitting on the table beside the bed.

There was no one in the room with her and the house was silent. She'd dreamed of him again. Not only that, but it had been more detailed, longer and more intense than the first. She trembled from the pleasure she'd never had but that still vibrated through her.

Lettie wouldn't admit it to anyone, not even Angeline, but she was scared. Her dreams were more like memories replaying themselves over and over. However, they weren't memories. She'd never done any of those things with any man, and certainly not with Shane Murphy.

Yet it was him in her dreams. It was him touching her, bringing her pleasure, making love to her. Confused thoughts bounced around in her head while her pussy still throbbed from the sex that didn't happen.

A few minutes later she rose from the bed to wash up. Nothing to clean off her but sweat, but it would help her get back to sleep. Although she wasn't sure that was a possibility. Heck, she might never sleep again.

After a quick, tepid wash, she pulled her night rail on, wondering if her knees would ever stop shaking. Lettie turned back toward the bed. Something small and dark lay on her pillow. She frowned, distracted by whatever it was. As she got closer, the shape became clear and she stopped dead in her tracks.

It was a sparrow feather.

How was it possible, in an empty room, in an empty house, that a sparrow feather, which had not been there three minutes ago, appeared?

The breeze from the open window danced across her skin, raising goose bumps. She stared at the curtains as they fluttered and wondered if she really had been alone and what the feather meant.

There would be no more sleep for Lettie that night.

Shane stared at his granny angel, dumbstruck by her offer. She could not possibly have meant what she said.

"You want me to work in the kitchen?" He frowned. "Me?"

"Angeline left us three months ago when she married Sam Carver. The girls, they try to help, but none of them can cook or bake." Marta pointed at him. "I heard what you said about the bread, Mr. Murphy. It was not good even if Lettie did her best."

Shane winced, unaware he had insulted Lettie with the comments about the bread. How was he to know she had baked it? The woman could not bake, that was for sure. Lettie obviously had plenty of other skills, like patching up drunk men.

"I still don't understand why you're offering me a job, Mrs. Gunderson." He gestured to his bandaged hands. "I don't think I can knead bread yet."

She waved her hand. "It will come in time. For now, you help me in the kitchen, ya? You can cut meat and potatoes into chunks. I see you eat. Your hands are better, almost healed."

He couldn't argue with her there. His hands were better, stiff and sore but no longer painful. He could take the bandages off and work. It would be the first honest job he'd had in a long time. He was suspicious, however, at the offer.

"They're better," he admitted. "But there has to be another girl in this town who needs a job. Why don't you hire a girl to work in the kitchen with you?"

"Bah, there is no one in town. I tried a couple girls, but they were worse than Lettie. I let them go back to their mamas to learn how to be women." Marta raised her brows. "You need a job, you live here, and you maybe find a home, ya?"

A home. It was a tempting offer, and he wondered how Lettie would react. She'd been right to push him away, to tell him they couldn't be together or have a future. Working at the Blue Plate might give him a chance to steal a few more minutes with her. It was a selfish reason, but then again so was contemplating accepting Mrs. Gunderson's proposal. There wasn't much in it for her. No doubt he ate a lot more than the other people who lived and worked at the restaurant.

Did he deserve what she offered? He'd had his fair share of heartache and pain, had spent time being punished for his sins. His gut told him to say no, to leave with the borrowed clothes and keep moving. His brain told him there wouldn't be another job like this one. Perhaps God was giving him a smidge of relief from his self-made hell.

The hard truth was, he had nowhere else to be and nothing else to do. He had been wandering from place to place with no destination. Being alone had become his standard way of existing. Being in the Blue Plate had forced him to remember what it was like to be around other people and not suffer his own company.

Marta watched him as he thought through the offer. She almost appeared smug as though she knew he would say yes. What other choice did he have?

"Okay, I'll work in your kitchen for you. I don't know how

long you're going to want me there, but I ain't got any pressing business to attend to right yet." He glanced down at his borrowed shirt and drawers, then at the trousers and shoes waiting for him. "I thank you for your loan of the clothes. Mine were apparently burned."

"Ah yes, they were not good." Marta made a face. "There were insects."

His cheeks heated at the embarrassing truth. He had been infested with all kinds of critters. After the bath Lettie gave him, the memory of how dirty he'd been had faded away. Until now.

"I'm right sorry about that, Mrs. Gunderson. I, um, was having some trouble keeping myself sober and clean." He straightened the blanket around him so he didn't have to look her in the face. "I surely appreciate everything you kind folks have done for me."

"We are nothing if we aren't kind, Mr. Murphy." Her words, an echo of Lettie's, told him exactly who had taught his wayward nurse about kindness. "I am happy to help when there is need. The trousers will be too short though. You are much taller than my Pieter. We will need to ask Sam if he has a pair you can use."

"Who's Sam?" The last thing he wanted was to be indebted to another stranger.

"Angeline's husband. You have met her?"

"No, I haven't. Lettie mentioned her though. She used to bake in the kitchen?" He didn't remember much else about her.

"She is Lettie's best friend. One day you will ask her about how they met and then you will know much about her." Marta got to her feet. "Tomorrow you will rise with me and start in the kitchen. Today I will find longer trousers for you to wear." She bent down and patted his cheek with her small, soft hand. "You are a good man, Mr. Murphy. You will do what's right."

With that cryptic statement, the older woman left him alone. He wondered if he had been talked into something that had already been decided upon before she walked in the room. If she thought he was a good man, she was sorely mistaken. He was anything but good. Judging by how much he'd taken advantage of their generosity, she should know that.

Yet this granny angel of his had decided he needed saving. Maybe it was in her nature to do so, as an angel of sorts. She expected a great deal from him, and he knew she would be disappointed when he didn't live up to those expectations. No doubt he would fall back into whiskey. After a week of being sober, the urge to find some was strong, a thirst deep within that scratched at him, needing to be quenched.

He wondered where the saloon was and how long it would take him to darken its door. When he did, Mrs. Gunderson and Lettie would give up on him. A drunk was a drunk. He couldn't change who he was, no matter how tempting the woman or the promise of what they might have found together.

They would discover quickly what he already knew. Shane Murphy was not a good man.

Chapter Four

Lettie didn't go back to Shane's room again on the day he was to leave. She was a coward, unable to face him knowing what she could never have. It left a bitter taste in her mouth she could not shake. The dreams bothered her, more than she wanted to admit to herself.

Then there was the sparrow feather, or rather feathers. When she'd woken that morning, she'd remembered the other one she'd found on the printing press. At the time, it hadn't meant a thing. Now there had been two feathers, inside a house with no birds or open windows. The mystery of how they got there knocked her sideways. There were strange goings-on in Forestville, and she wanted no part of it.

She'd spent Friday evening printing the paper. The smell, the sound, the satisfaction of the end result was enough to distract her, even from her weeping heart.

In the morning, she delivered a stack of the weekly paper to the general store to sell then made her way to the Blue Plate. Every Saturday she had ink-stained hands and had to scrub them with lye before she started serving meals. Marta insisted on having clean hands to work in the restaurant, which wasn't a bad thing. It was a tough chore this Saturday though. The printing press had been particularly ornery this week, and she had more stains than usual.

She went around the back of the building to use the sink in the kitchen. Marta would expect her to be working in less than ten minutes. Lettie hurried up the steps and burst into the room.

"I'm not late yet. I need to wash the ink—" She paused, completely flummoxed by the sight that met her eyes. At first she thought she was still dreaming, or the ink had turned her brain cockeyed.

Shane.

Vivid snatches of her dreams slammed into her, and she couldn't catch her breath. Yet he was real this time. He stood at the big butcher-block counter, flour covering his hands and arms, wearing an apron with lace edging. Marta was next to him, sprinkling more flour on the dough in front of them. She looked up and smiled at Lettie.

"Good morning, *liebchen.* You are not late yet. You'd best scrub those hands though. You know the rules." Marta turned her attention back to Shane. "Now I massage the flour into the dough. This part might hurt your fingers."

Lettie couldn't find her voice, shock keeping her tongue still. What in the hell was Shane doing making bread dough in the kitchen? He was supposed to be gone. Gone! Why was he still there? This wouldn't do at all. He couldn't be around or she'd never stop dreaming about him and his touch. Even now, her body reacted to being in the same room with him. Oh no, it couldn't happen. He must not stay.

Shane hadn't even turned his head toward her, other than a passing glance when she first came into the kitchen. She didn't know what hurt worse—his presence or his apparent lack of interest in her. Lettie dug deep and yanked on her mental bootstraps until she could speak again.

"What is happening here?"

Marta stopped and looked at her. "We are making bread."

"I can see you're making bread. I'm not stupid, Marta. What is *he* doing in the kitchen?" She snapped at him, "Why aren't you gone?"

He flinched a bit. "Nice to know I made a good impression on you, Lettie."

"Miss Brown if you don't mind." Now that she'd started talking, she couldn't seem to stop. Her tongue knew no bounds when her temper took over. "You told me you were leaving."

His long fingers flipped the dough, and he used his palms to massage in the flour. "I changed my mind when Mrs. Gunderson offered me a job."

She gaped. "Marta! What were you thinking in hiring him? A week ago he was puking on my shoes, which, by the way, are still stained."

Marta's expression hardened. "This is not your place to question who I hire. Pieter and I own the Blue Plate. We needed someone in the kitchen, and Mr. Murphy knows how to make bread."

Fury rushed through her, unwanted and unheeded. Lettie felt as though her head was going to explode. There was no reason for her to be angry, but she was. Last night she had come to terms with not seeing Shane again. Now she found him working in the very kitchen she had to enter dozens and dozens of times each day.

It could not happen.

"You can't hire him."

Marta wiped her hands on a rag and walked over to the stove. "I have already done so. Mr. Murphy has been working for two hours now."

"Then unhire him." Lettie knew she was being unreasonable, but she couldn't stop herself. She was tumbling down the hill and picking up speed. "I can't work here if he is here."

"You're being foolish, Lettie." Marta had never raised her voice before. "And rude. Mr. Murphy has done nothing to hurt you."

Oh, yes he had, but not in the way Marta would understand. He had dredged up feelings and sensations Lettie didn't know she had and didn't want. She felt excitement, arousal and worst of all, a smidge of joy. Now she couldn't forget all of that, not with him around her constantly. It would be like rubbing salt in an open wound every single day.

She couldn't do it. She just couldn't.

"Then I quit."

Marta's mouth dropped open. "*Liebchen*, you cannot mean that."

Lettie's eyes stung, and she blinked away the pain. Her hands clenched into fists, the nails digging into her palms.

Shane finally looked at her again. "Lettie, I can—"

"Don't you let her run you off, Mr. Murphy. Lettie cannot bully everyone into doing her bidding." Marta slammed the spoon against the stove. "She needs to wash her hands and get to work now. I am done talking about this."

The silence hung heavy in the room, the burble of the pot on the stove the only sound other than Lettie's blood thumping through her ears. She shouldn't be so angry because Marta gave the man a job. There was no logical reason for her reaction. Yet she also couldn't stop her fury. It had a life of its own.

"I will go wash my hands outside." Lettie snatched the lye soap, scrub brush and a rag from the sink and slammed out the door. The summer heat closed in around her, making her feel hotter than she already was.

She felt sick, queasy enough to see the biscuit she'd eaten

earlier. Swallowing hard, she walked to the well pump, her legs stiff. Her world had been flipped upside down, once more, by a man. Shane wasn't just any man though. He was the man who made her feel.

Lettie pumped the handle harder than necessary, a growl hiding in her throat. She pulled the lye across the brush bristles, wincing when some landed near her eye. It was unthinkable, unacceptable that she was so out of control.

"Lettie."

Shane's voice forced the growl out of her. "Get away from me, Shane."

"I'm sorry me being here made you so angry. I told Marta I would leave. I don't want you to quit your job." He sounded contrite and sincere, damn him.

"Why would you leave? You have nowhere to go." She scrubbed her hands, ignoring the pain from the rough brush.

"It doesn't matter. I had nowhere to go before I came here." The life she'd seen and heard from within him was gone, extinguished by her righteous fury.

Lettie shook with the emotions flowing through her. She knew she had to do the right thing. It wasn't fair to him to suffer the wrath of an irrational woman who spent many days wondering if she was loco.

"No, don't leave. I'll learn to ignore you, and we'll get along fine." Sometimes she wished she could seal her mouth closed. The words that came out managed to hurt someone every time she spoke.

"That's what you want?"

"No, but I reckon I will accept it." She rinsed her hands off, setting the brush and soap on the wood beside the pump. As she dried her hands, she could not bring herself to look at

Shane. "You'd best get back in there and finish making the bread. We don't want to serve any that tastes like old shoes again."

The moment was pregnant with unsaid words. She continued to dry her hands, waiting until he left her alone. When she heard footsteps moving away from her, Lettie let out the breath she was holding.

What was she going to do? Shane was going to be there every day, every moment.

His heart pumped a steady rhythm, a pace that increased with each passing moment. It was her. She drove him loco, turned him into a panting fool. He could not resist her, ever. All she had to do was crook her finger and he jumped to attention. Tonight was no exception.

They were alone, the quiet music of the night surrounding them. He watched her undress, each piece of clothing revealing another glorious part of her. In the lamplight, her skin glowed like cream, waiting to be licked and tasted. He shifted on the bed, needing to touch his woman. She was teasing him deliberately, and while he loved it, he could hardly stand another minute. Yet he would because he needed to.

Down to her chemise, she strutted back and forth, her breasts bouncing softly beneath the fabric. His mouth watered, eager to taste. She reached up and unpinned her hair, sending a zing of arousal straight through him. He loved her hair. The dark locks tumbled down, swaying against the cotton fabric with a swish. He clenched his hands, remembering the feel of her hair against his chest, his stomach, his thighs. Her long hair fell almost to the round cheeks of her ass. The sweet globes were just right for squeezing and holding on as he plunged into her.

"Take it off." His voice had become gravelly with need.

She stopped her antics long enough to raise one brow at him. Shit. She would tease him further now. What kind of idiot prolonged his own agony? One who couldn't be quiet. He wouldn't tell her how much he wanted her. Hell, he didn't have to. All she had to do was look at his too-tight drawers and the hunger on his face.

With a grin, she slowly slid the chemise up her thighs. His pulse notched up when he saw the shadow of her pussy, then she turned around and revealed that perfectly round ass again. A groan crept up his throat, but he didn't let it loose. No need to let her know her underhanded tactics were working, even if his dick was hard enough to hammer a nail.

The chemise went higher and higher until it reached her shoulders. The garment slid off, the sound of the fabric against her skin almost loud in the quiet room. She pulled her hair forward and turned.

"Damn." The word slipped out before he could stop it.

She smiled, the wench. Her hair covered those glorious tits, and her hands covered the pussy he wanted so very much to see. She inched closer, revealing one rose-colored nipple between the strands before she shifted again and hid the precious peak.

"You are going to kill me."

She laughed, a husky sound that sent a shiver up his spine. "You would die a happy man."

That was true. She had become a fever in his blood, one that would never be quenched. He was obsessed, plain and simple.

She moved closer to the bed, close enough he could almost

touch her. She swayed back and forth as though dancing to music only she could hear. He watched, fascinated, as she spread her legs, revealing the pink folds of her core. Her musky scent called to him, drawing him near. His mouth watered in anticipation, impatient and needy.

He fell to his belly and reached for her. "Let me taste you, honey. I gotta taste you."

Obviously taking pity on him, she spread her pussy lips, and he saw how wet she was. Her play excited both of them, which only made him harder. His dick throbbed against the sheets, eager for more than cotton. First he had to taste her.

He leaned forward and licked her pussy from top to bottom. As a shiver raced through him, her body quaked too. They were connected at an elemental level, by everything they did, felt or sensed. He'd never known such a bond existed between a man and a woman. Finding it with her, by accident or design, was more than a gift.

Like a bee too long denied its nectar, he lapped at her, the sweet tang of her arousal coating his tongue. She made kittenish moans in her throat as he sucked on her clit. He felt her racing pulse through the tender skin. When he reached to put two fingers inside her, she stepped back, his mouth making a smacking sound as the treat was pulled away.

"Please, honey." He was too aroused to be embarrassed at begging.

She shook her head and pointed at the bed, her breathing uneven, a sheen of perspiration on her skin. Damned if she didn't look like a goddess come to life, aroused, beautiful, and all his. Her brown eyes glowed with heat, and her hair held its own power, its waves curling around her body like he wanted to.

He lay back, shucking his drawers since there was no

pretense any longer. He wanted her, he needed her, he was hers to do with as she wished. A fantastic fate to have. One he would be eternally grateful for.

She leaned forward and licked his dick once, sucking the head of it into the recesses of her mouth. He almost came on the spot. Fisting his fingers into the linens, he hung on, counting to ten over and over again until she let his staff go with an audible pop.

Grinning, she climbed onto the bed, straddling him. She pulled her hair back, revealing the tits he so desperately needed to suck. He reached for her, and she allowed him to cup the orbs and feel their weight in his hands.

She hovered over him, the heat from her pussy tickling his skin. He swore his dick tried to jump up those three inches to touch her. She braced herself on his chest, her nipples swaying close but not close enough for him to taste.

He tried though, more than once. She grinned and dangled one right over his mouth. As he captured the nipple with a groan, she grabbed his dick and aimed it right into her core. Slowly, ever so slowly, she sank down on his length.

His teeth closed around the nipple, and he hung on to his control by a thread. She moaned her approval, and he nibbled at her again. By the time he was fully sheathed inside her, he was shaking with restraint. He needed to fuck her hard and fast, feel the heat between them burst into white-hot passion.

Yet this was her game, hers to control. He'd promised her he'd let her hold the reins that night, which he now regretted. It was more difficult than anything he'd ever done, and it was only love that helped maintain that thread of control.

She closed her eyes and sat up, yanking the precious nipple from his mouth. Like a lovesick fool, he whimpered. This time she was too caught up in what she was doing to tease him any longer. She threw her head back and braced her hands on his chest, pulling herself up until he was nearly free of her wet heat, then slammed down on him.

His brain ceased to function at all the second time she did it. He hung on to her hips, eager for more, guiding her path. Selfish, but so goddamn good. Her pussy tightened around him with each downward stroke, pulling him with her as she rose up again.

She wanted to ride him, to be in charge of their lovemaking. How could he resist her? He would give his life for her. Why not give her the reins in their bed too? He should regret it, but it felt so damn good, enough to make him want to do it again and again.

Her face was a study in beauty, her lips parted, breathy moans emanating from them each time he pushed deep inside her. Her eyes were half closed, their depths whirling with passion and pleasure. Her skin was soft and hot to the touch, his hand sliding over her hips to her thighs then back.

He was fast losing the battle to keep his orgasm at bay. His balls tightened to the point of pain, and he knew he was only moments away from exploding, but he wouldn't go without his woman. He reached between them to find her clit, the nubbin swollen and slick in the folds of her pussy.

As he flicked it, she clenched harder, the walls of her cunt impossibly strong. He started coming before he could stop it. She screamed his name, and together they rode the waves of ecstasy. He gripped her hips, plunging deep, deep, deep inside her. She hung on to his arms, her body quivering around his.

For a moment, he was lost in a whirlwind so intense, he forgot where he was. Her body collapsed against his, her heart beating like a rabbit. Her hair surrounded them, cocooning them as the waves subsided. He touched her head, running his fingers through the soft waves, his throat tight with emotion.

"I love you, Lettie."

Shane woke up, sweating and aching. His dick was harder than an oak tree, pulsing against his drawers. He had never had a more realistic dream in his life. Her scent clung to the air around him, a musky perfume he knew was uniquely hers.

Another dream. About her. This time he'd spoken her name in the dream. Jesus Christ, he could hardly believe how realistic the dreams were. He'd memorized her body, her pleasure spots, the taste of her pussy. It was impossible to know any of it, yet he did, as though he'd been with her for years.

He wasn't about to go back to sleep. In fact, he would have to get rid of the erection or he might never sleep again. It had been some time since he'd had a stiff dick. Now he'd had one twice since meeting Lettie.

Closing his eyes, he pictured her face as it was in the dream. Mouth open, eyes languid with deep passion, her breasts shining with perspiration and her hot channel wrapped around him. It took only half a dozen strokes before he came so hard he saw stars.

More than embarrassed, he got to his feet and washed up quickly, including wiping the sweat off his body. The breeze through the open window ruffled the curtains, drying his overheated skin. He yanked his drawers on and was climbing into bed when he spotted something on his pillow.

A feather.

He picked it up, twirling it between his fingers. It appeared to be a sparrow feather. How had it gotten in the room, and why was it on his pillow? He set it on the windowsill, somehow more disturbed than he should be by an innocuous item like a feather.

He finally climbed into bed, restless and more than anxious. The dream hung on him like a heavy coat, the details so incredibly real, he could almost taste her cunt on his tongue. Whatever had happened in the dream, it hadn't happened in this room. It was a house he'd never been in yet he knew it as though he lived there.

What did it mean? He dreamed, of course, like everyone. But this had been more like a memory, which was ridiculous because he'd never done more than kiss Lettie. He certainly hadn't made love to her or tasted her nectar. Lord only knew if her body was as he imagined it, although he wouldn't be surprised if she was built like he expected.

An owl hooted outside the window. Shane lay there for hours, sleep eluding him, remembering each moment of his dream. The next time he saw Lettie, his dream would rush back at him. But it hadn't been real no matter how much he wished it was.

Shane kept repeating it to himself, but it didn't matter. He felt the ghost of her fingers on him, smelled her unique scent and tasted her tang on his tongue.

He was in trouble.

A week passed. Shane had done his best to avoid Lettie as much as she avoided him. It pained him to do so, but there was no help for it. He knew if he saw her his dick would harden and she would hate him worse than she already did. God, she was going to quit rather than see him. He'd had erotic dreams four times already. Pretty soon he would have a rash from masturbating too much. It was embarrassing and frustrating.

He was stronger though, and the swelling around his eye was gone. The stitches needed to come out, but he couldn't ask Lettie to do it. In a few days he'd break down and ask someone because they were starting to itch. His physical injuries were healing, helped by the good food and sleep he was getting. If only his heart and his gut would get better. He craved the two things he couldn't and shouldn't have—Lettie and whiskey.

Both of them were trouble, and he needed to steer clear. Yet at night he dreamed of one and thirsted for the other. It was driving him loco, and he had to find a way to forget both of them. He nearly snorted at the thought, as though it was that easy.

Shane had settled into working in the kitchen. He made all the baked goods and helped Marta as much as he could. This morning she was flustered and running around like a little bird with her tail feathers ruffled. Shane kept his eyes down and pretended not to notice.

"I need those supplies, or we won't be able to cook in two days." Marta fussed over the stove, her normally perfectly styled grayish-blonde hair in a puffy halo around her head. "The store has no flour, sugar, salt or beans. How can I do anything without the staples?"

Pieter stood in the kitchen, his arms crossed, a scowl on his face. "What do you wish me to do, Marta? I have asked for the supplies, but they no deliver. The man who drive freight wagon, he crashed and died last week."

News to Shane and startling at that. The man who had likely beat him nearly to death had died in a crash in the same wagon that had brought Shane to Forestville. Was it just punishment for a man who deserved it? Or a coincidence? Either way, he was glad to hear it, selfishly so. The freight wagon driver may have beaten Shane, and only the luck of Lettie's intervention had saved him. If the stranger hadn't beaten Shane, the driver had left him barely alive at the Blue Plate without helping Shane. Maybe it was all part of a big plan, and he was a pawn unable to make his own move.

Marta looked over at Shane who was making biscuits. "Perhaps Mr. Murphy can go to Benson for the supplies, ya? Borrow a wagon."

Shane was startled and stared at the Gundersons as they discussed sending him to another town for supplies. Alone. Where there were saloons and whiskey to be had.

He licked his lips, a cramp of thirst gripping his belly. They couldn't possibly mean to give him this responsibility when he wasn't two weeks without a drink. It would be madness, and he sure as hell would never make it back to the Blue Plate.

"This is good. Ya, this is good." Pieter looked at Shane, his bushy eyebrows beetled together into a V. "I ask Lettie to go with him. Together they can bring back the supplies."

"Lettie? She can't stand to be in the same room with me," Shane blurted. "I don't think this is a good idea."

"There is no one else. Karen has to take care of Dennis, and Alice, she does not work so hard." Pieter nodded. "Sam has to stay to take care of our Angeline since she is with child. My hands are too crooked now to help. That leaves Lettie. She is strong and good worker."

It was logical to pick her. Logic be damned, it wasn't going to work. Sitting next to her on a wagon seat, he'd be able to smell her, to feel her heat, to get lost in the fake memories he had of making love to her. Shane broke out in a sweat, panic flirting at the edge of his mind.

"She won't go," Shane reiterated. "I'm sure of it."

"Oh, she will go." Marta's face was set with determination.

"Lettie will help the restaurant no matter her foolish notions. We need her help."

"I can go by myself." Was he a complete idiot? He couldn't possibly go by himself, and if he did, he'd end up at the bottom of a whiskey barrel.

"No, you are not healed enough to go alone. You need help." Marta crossed her arms and frowned. "The only thing you do now is make bread and biscuits. This is not heavy or hard. Driving a wagon is hard, and you need a partner."

A partner. He'd had a partner once, or thought he had, and now she was gone, laid in the earth to become part of it again. Shane would never have another partner. His heart had died with the first, and there was nothing left inside him. The Gundersons couldn't possibly know that, of course, and he wasn't going to share the story of his loss. Seven years later, it was a knife buried in his gut, festering and bleeding.

"Then it's settled. They will leave in the morning."

Marta's pronouncement startled Shane. While he'd been thinking, she and Pieter had convinced each other the plan was sound. Shane was helpless as a leaf in a swollen creek, barreling along toward a fifty-foot waterfall. The trip would be a disaster. He could feel it. Didn't they realize how untrustworthy he was? Or how much Lettie didn't want to be near him?

She would refuse to go. He could feel it in his bones.

Lettie stared out the window of the restaurant. The predawn grayness outside matched her mood. The day would be painful, but she would endure it because the Gundersons needed her. Marta told her the restaurant would suffer without her help, to the point they would lose customers and perhaps several days of income.

She had said no more than once, but Marta kept asking and asking until finally Lettie relented. Since then, the thought of spending the day beside Shane on a wagon seat, alone, had made her break out in a sweat.

It would be excruciatingly awkward, but Lettie would endure. That was what she did best—endure. She'd lasted through five years of marriage to a monster. One trip to buy supplies with a man who offered her the promise of an empty future could be done. Lettie knew she should not be distressed about the trip, but her gut and her heart told her different.

Loathe to admit it to herself, Lettie had begun to daydream about the night dreams she had of him. Perversely, she wanted to have another night dream. She wanted to feel it all again, even if it had been conjured by her own imagination.

She had resigned herself to keeping distance between them, ignored him with every bit of her. He needed to pick up and move on. She struggled to maintain disinterest and at the same time wanted to know more about him. She wanted to ask him about the scar on his shoulder, the other one on his stomach, the mole on his back, and the strawberry birthmark at the base of his neck. Unfortunately for her she had cataloged every inch of him during his bath. Each tiny detail appeared in her dreams as well. Her lips had kissed the scars, her tongue had licked them. She closed her eyes, remembering the salty flavor of his skin that she had never truly tasted.

Lettie was losing the battle with her determination to forget Shane and everything they had done or said. He was a constant reminder of what she couldn't have. Now Marta had talked her into spending the day, the *entire* day, in his company, alone. If she didn't know any better, she might have suspected the older woman of conspiring to put them together.

However, Lettie knew the freight wagon had been damaged

when the driver was killed, and supplies were very thin at the store. She'd been in there two days ago, and the shelves were looking bare. Even the cracker barrel had been almost empty. Nearly as empty as her heart.

"Lettie?"

She turned around to find Angeline by the door, her brow furrowed and concern evident on her face. "Marta told me about the supply trip."

Lettie knew her friend understood how uncomfortable the experience would be. Angeline crossed the room, weaving her way through the tables and chairs until she reached the window. She wore a beautiful blue dress, and Lettie had a crazy notion she wanted one just like it instead of her usual brown. However, a woman like Lettie didn't wear bright colors.

Angeline leaned against the windowpane, her arms crossed. "Let Sam go in your place."

"No, that ain't right. He needs to be here for you. It's only a one-day trip. It's not like I'm running off for a month with Sha—with a man. I'll be fine." Lettie's words sounded weak like the big fat fib they were.

Angeline shook her head. "You are a terrible liar."

Lettie managed to shrug off her friend's concern. "I do what I need to."

"Marta shouldn't have pushed you to go. It's too much to ask." Angeline sounded guilty yet she had no reason to be. Lettie had made her choice.

"I would do anything for the Gundersons." The truth, at last. Although she knew it would be hell on earth, Lettie would do what was asked because she owed the couple so much. Her life, her job, her future.

"Me too." Angeline looked as though she wanted to hug

Lettie but kept her distance. "I would also do anything for you."

Lettie's throat tightened, and she had to shake off the impending cloud of dark emotions. Now was not the time for them. "You already have. Let's not get all sappy and stupid."

"I'll think about it." Angeline grinned, coaxing an answering one from Lettie.

The phrase was one they'd repeated to each other during their journey from Utah to Wyoming. It kept them alive and awake when they were running and hiding. No one but Angeline would understand their relationship or how much they had survived because of it.

"I'd best go get moving before the sun gets too hot." Lettie knew her friend was there out of concern, but she was done talking about it. Hell she'd spent the entire night thinking about the day ahead. Now she wanted to get it over with so she could forget it.

Liar.

She didn't know what she wanted. Spending the day with the man who haunted her dreams was what would happen.

Shane walked into the room dressed in the same outfit he wore every day. It reminded her of how little he had, only one set of clothes, ones that didn't belong to him. Although he hadn't said anything, she was fairly certain the boots were too small. The man had big feet and Pieter did not.

Angeline raised one blonde brow at Lettie, her expression surprised and curious. Oh hell, now she would have to introduce them. She didn't want her friend meddling in this business, but she couldn't very well be rude and not introduce them. Actually she could, but she wouldn't out of respect for Angeline.

"Shane Murphy, this here is Mrs. Angeline Carver." The introduction was as flat as her enthusiasm for the day's events.

Shane surprised her by taking off his hat and nodding to Angeline. "It's a pleasure to meet you, Mrs. Carver. I've heard a lot about you from the ladies here at the restaurant."

"Really? I've heard very little about you." She grinned at Lettie then turned to Shane. "I'm so pleased to see you're healing well after your injuries. Our Lettie is a miracle worker."

"I'll second that." A frown creased his brow. "She did a right kind thing by taking care of me. I'll never forget her."

His words skittered down her spine, their double meaning raising every small hair on her body. She wanted so badly to throw caution to the wind and kiss him. But she didn't and she wouldn't. What she'd told him a week ago was still the truth. She could never be the woman he needed. As far as Lettie was concerned, nothing would change that.

Angeline looked between them. "Interesting."

"Stop it, Angeline."

"Stop what? I didn't do anything. It was a pleasure to meet you, Mr. Murphy. I can see why you have all the ladies in a tizzy here." With another grin for Lettie, she walked toward the front of the restaurant. "Try not to kill each other. Blood will ruin the flour."

Shane scowled. "Blood will ruin the flour?"

"She's expecting, and it's made her act foolish." Lettie snatched up the basket of food on the table beside her. "Let's get going then. Sooner started, sooner finished."

She tried not to notice his scent or his nearness as she passed within inches of him. The man stood in her path, after all, and he wasn't being polite and moving out of her way. She stuck her nose in the air, her anger simmering at Angeline, at Shane and most of all, at herself. The entire situation was her own fault, and she'd have to muddle her way through it.

He touched her elbow, and she flinched. A breath hissed through his teeth, but he didn't say anything. She kept walking, wondering if life would ever be anything but painful. She had reached a point where she was content, and now emotions were turning her inside out again. Damn the man for falling onto her shoes. She'd never forgive him for it.

The wagon was ready and waiting outside the restaurant. The rig and the horses had been rented from the livery in town, costing the Gundersons money. Yet she knew others in town had contributed some, asking for supplies of their own. Lettie had a hefty list of goods to purchase, and she hoped the store in Benson had everything she needed.

Without waiting for assistance, she climbed into the wagon and settled onto the seat. The wood creaked and popped as Shane hoisted himself up beside her. He didn't say a thing, but his thigh settled inches from hers. Feeling petty but unable to help herself, she pulled her skirt closer so it didn't touch him.

What was wrong with her? He was a seemingly good man, who for some unknown reason found her attractive, and she pushed him away. It wasn't logical, and she could hardly explain it to herself. Here they sat, uncomfortable and out of sorts, barely speaking. It seemed like a lifetime ago she'd bathed his body and they'd kissed. In the days since then, she had dreamed of making love with him.

A twister roared through her, tying her up into tight little knots she couldn't possibly undo. Sitting there as uncomfortable as she'd expected, even more so. She counted each clop of the horses' hooves as each second ticked by. It helped pass the time and gave her something to do besides be silent and awkward.

By the time she reached two thousand four hundred and thirty, she was gritting her teeth. She could swear Shane was deliberately inching closer to her. The metal handle on the seat was currently digging into her hip.

At six thousand two hundred and fifty, she gave up counting entirely. Her hip was throbbing, she had to pee and she had swallowed a bug. It was time to stop and rest for a few minutes.

"Stop the wagon."

"Huh?" He turned to her, as though he had been daydreaming about anything but sitting beside her on a wagon.

"Stop. The. Wagon. I need to, ah, use the necessary." Lettie refused to say please. That was not in her vocabulary anymore when she spoke to men, any man.

"Oh, sure thing. I could stretch my legs too after the last couple hours."

"A couple hours? It's only been a couple hours?" She punched him in the arm.

"Ow." He pulled the wagon to a stop in a grassy area and set the brake. As he rubbed the spot where she'd punched him, he scowled at her from under the brim of his borrowed flat-brimmed brown hat. "Why did you hit me?"

Lettie stared, horrified by the fact she had punched him. The man had been beaten nearly to death, and she knew very well how much fists hurt, far longer than the bruises lasted. Yet she had deliberately hit him.

"I'm sorry." Her voice was barely above a whisper. When he opened his mouth to respond, she turned and leapt off the wagon. She landed hard on her right ankle, which then throbbed as she tottered off to the nearby bushes to relieve herself.

Lettie was never this out of sorts. She felt itchy, as though she could jump out of her skin any minute. As she found a suitable bush, she pulled up her skirt and did what she needed to. She never forgot for a second that Shane was close enough to hear her urinate. It was another strange thing about a strange day.

By the time she cleaned herself up and straightened her clothes, she had calmed down sufficiently to return to the wagon. Her swollen ankle complained with each step, and her boot was too tight. The day kept getting worse.

Shane leaned against the side of the wagon, his feet crossed at the ankle, a stalk of grass stuck between his teeth. He watched her approach, his face hidden by the shade of his hat so she couldn't see his eyes. She didn't like that one bit.

"What's wrong with your foot?"

"Nothing. I twisted it a bit is all." She went around the back of the wagon and reached into the basket for a bite to eat. With her stomach jumping like a passel of frogs, she didn't need to get sick from having no food.

"Is there enough in there for me?"

"No."

"You sure are being ornery, Lettie." Shane wasn't accusatory, but he was annoying.

"Then you know the real me." She found a ham biscuit and turned her back to him. No need to flaunt the food at him—she wasn't that mean. It wasn't because she didn't want to look at him. Or at least that was what she told herself.

"No, but I'm waiting to meet her." Shane's response made her pause in mid-motion.

She swung around and speared him with a glare. "What do you mean by that?"

He shrugged. "Just that. You don't let anyone see you, Lettie."

His words hit her square between the eyes. It was the truth, of course, but painful nonetheless. She managed not to spit out the bite in her mouth that had turned to ash on her tongue. Lettie swallowed what she could to save herself from looking foolish. Her hands shook with anger.

A little voice deep inside told her it was fear.

"That's none of your business, Mr. Murphy. You don't mean anything to me."

"I know that."

"You are a drunk, a stranger who puked on my shoes and nothing more."

"I know that."

She was within a foot of him, her sharp words whipping through the air like knives. He didn't flinch or move as she beat him with her verbal fury. Her chest heaved as she struggled for breath, overwhelmed and out of control.

"You are here out of pity. Marta and Pieter felt sorry for you. You aren't part of our family and you never will be." Her mouth fairly burned with the viciousness of her attack.

"I know that."

"Stop saying that." She thumped one fist on his chest, then the other. Soon she was punching him for all she was worth. Her throat burned, her eyes shed angry tears and she let loose a torrent of sobs that sounded more like a wounded animal than a woman.

Lettie lost all sense of time and self. She tumbled down into a dark, deep hole and huddled there. Strong arms surrounded her, keeping her from sinking any further. Soft crooning echoed in her ear while warm hands rubbed her back.

She couldn't tell how much time had passed before she realized she was curled into a ball on someone's lap. A male lap.

Her arms and legs were stiff, her face hot and wet. She shifted, flush with embarrassment over her attack on him and her subsequent fit. Angeline was the only one who knew about them. Until now.

His arm tightened around her shoulders. "Sit."

"I can't sit on your lap, Shane." She got to her feet, her legs trembling. When she took a step, she lost her balance and fell. He caught her in midair, his arm pushing the breath out of her lungs.

"I reckon you'll sit now." He flipped her around, and she found herself right back in his lap.

She should have gotten up, should have told him to let her go, but she didn't. The sad truth was, he was comfortable, he smelled good and she didn't want to move. Normally after losing control like that, she felt sick the rest of the day. Shane's presence must have kept that sickness at bay because her stomach wasn't hurting in the least.

"I, uh, I'm sorry about what I did." The apology was like sawdust in her mouth, dry and tasteless.

"You don't need to apologize." His voice was honey smooth in her ear.

"Yes I do. I didn't mean to. I've been having fits for a while. I can't rightly control it." Her cheeks burned as she admitted there was something very wrong with her.

"I get that way too with whiskey," he admitted. "I have days, hell weeks, I don't remember."

She knew whiskey could make a man stupid but didn't know it could snatch days from his memory. Another reason not to drink a drop of it. She wondered if Shane would fall back into the bottle again or if he could resist the lure of its amber depths. Lettie didn't have a choice when it involved her black periods, but maybe he didn't either.

The sounds of life surrounded them, birds sang, squirrels chattered and bees buzzed. The sun shone brightly on the meadow while Shane and Lettie sat in the shadow of the wagon. It seemed only they knew how dark life could be.

Although she wouldn't admit it, Lettie wanted to sit there for as long as she could. Common sense told her that wasn't possible and she really needed to stop sitting on his lap. Marta would chastise her while Pieter would likely box Shane's ears for touching her.

Without a word, she finally moved, rolling to her knees. He steadied her as she rose and straightened her skirt. There were smears of dirt on the brown fabric, not that it made much difference. She didn't dress to be pretty, and most days the brown she owned suited her fine. Her heart might not bear it if she did wear a bright blue dress like Angeline.

The sound of a creek or stream nearby reminded her she needed to wash her face. It felt tight and sticky after her stupid crying. She walked on stiff legs toward the water, leaving Shane behind.

The peaceful-looking stream was a welcome sight. She knelt and cupped the water in her hands. First to splash on her face, then to take a long drink. The cool water tasted wonderful and felt even better. She sat there, listening to the gurgle of the stream, and wished she could find the same calmness nature had given the little oasis. She was more like a raging storm, wreaking havoc and tossing everything about. The fit she'd pitched made her sick. Knowing Shane had witnessed it was worse.

"We should get going." His voice made her start. "We still have at least three hours to go."

She accepted his help again getting to her feet, and they walked back to the wagon together. The water had given her the calming moment she needed. The rest of the trip had to be better than the first part. She wouldn't be counting hoofbeats this time either.

When she took Shane's hand to step up into the wagon, Lettie realized she had never felt so out of character. He turned her into a lady, strange as that was. When he sat beside her, she didn't shy away from him. Theirs was a comfortable distance, yet not close enough to touch.

The next hour passed quickly. Lettie watched Shane out of the corner of her eye, impressed by how well he handled the team. His hands fascinated her, ever since she'd dreamed of how they felt on her body.

Lettie wondered if she would feel the same pleasure in reality, if those hands were as skilled. Her stomach fluttered at the thought. And then it lurched in surprise when she flew through the air, thrown from the wagon, and landed in the dirt with a bone-jarring thud. The horses let loose horrible pained whinnies, and a series of cracks echoed across the ground. Lettie couldn't get her breath in or move.

Then the wagon landed on her legs and she screamed.

Chapter Five

Shane rolled when he hit the ground, and the hard, pebble-strewn prairie tore into his knees and hips. Pain roared through him as the borrowed trousers ripped. Warm blood trickled down his skin as he tried to catch his breath.

He knew something had gone horribly wrong with the wagon. The horses were making a god-awful noise, and the wagon creaked and cracked like an old man's back. Over the whinnies, he heard another sound, one that made his blood run cold.

Lettie was screaming.

Regardless that he was hurt and the fact he couldn't breathe, Shane scrambled to his feet and turned to see a horror. The wheel had splintered, sending the entire wagon careening forward until the corner hit the ground and it flipped. The back end had twisted sideways and landed on Lettie, who lay prone beneath it.

He ignored the horses and their sharp hooves, maneuvering around them until he reached Lettie. His heart pounded so hard, it damn near broke his ribs. Blood decorated her face and neck, the bun at the back of her hair nearly undone by the force of her fall.

"Jesus Christ." He dropped to his knees. His own injuries made him grimace, but he didn't care one whit. The wagon had her pinned beneath it. He tried to lift it up, but it didn't budge an inch. The horses yanked and tugged in their desperate attempt to escape. When they dragged the broken mess a few inches in their struggle, Lettie screamed again.

He touched her shoulder, afraid to cause her any more pain than she was already in. "I've got to get the horses loose."

"Hurry the hell up." Her voice was rough and breathless, but he was glad to hear her speak.

Shane scrambled toward the horses to find them caught up in the traces. One of them had a broken leg, the shiny, bloody bone poking through the dark brown pelt. He wished he had a gun—he had nothing but his hands. Shane attacked the harnesses, yanking on them until his hands bled. The leather was old and cracked, but it would not give way.

He resorted to using his teeth, tearing at the foul-tasting traces until they started to loosen. Inch by painful inch, Lettie's screams echoing in his ears, he freed one horse, then the other. Using strength he couldn't possibly have, he heaved and tugged at the horses' bits until they stood, completely free from the wagon's snare. The one with the broken leg fell almost instantly, its pitiful cry sounding more like a wounded child's. He had to ignore any pity for the animal and think about Lettie.

"Shane!" Her voice was full of agony, sending shards of panic into his heart.

He got back up and surveyed the wreck for a lever. Something to help him lift the wagon and release Lettie. One large piece had almost snapped free from the side of the wagon. He bent it back and forth until it came completely off. It wasn't as thick as he would have liked, but it was all he had unless he figured out a way to chop down a tree with his bare hands.

Shane dug under the side of the wagon until he thought the lever was positioned well enough to leverage it up. Sweat ran down his back in a river. Somewhere along the way, he'd lost his hat, and he tasted blood on his tongue. He wiped the sweat off his forehead with his sleeve, making his eyes sting more.

Her screams had stopped, and he assumed she had passed out, which was a good thing because she couldn't feel the pain. She might be dead. Fear made his stomach ball up into a knot, leaving behind an icy panic.

She is not dead. Not dead.

"Hold fast, Lettie. I'm almost there." His voice was as rough as the rest of him, raw and pained.

He maneuvered the wood under the wagon and slowly pushed. The wagon creaked and groaned, and it moved a few inches up. He glanced at Lettie, but she was still. There wasn't enough room for him to reach down and pull her legs out. He had to lever it up higher.

Shane wiggled the wood farther in, until it was nearly halfway under. This time, he heaved with all his might. The wagon rose half a foot. He squatted, bracing the wood with his back, using every ounce of strength he had to keep the wagon up. Splinters dug into his shoulder as he stretched out and snagged her skirt, pulling as hard as he could. All but her left foot was clear.

He was fairly certain she'd want to keep that foot so he pulled harder, but his own foot blocked hers.

"Goddammit!" He had no choice but to raise the wagon up farther and move farther under. He scooted backwards and pushed again, his muscles screaming in agony. He shook with exhaustion, holding the weight of the entire wagon on his back. Closer to Lettie, he caught her shoelace with one finger and yanked until she was finally free of the wagon.

With a ragged breath he set the ruined wagon on the ground then collapsed beside it. His breath came out in gusts as he tried to get his wind back. After a few moments, he rolled to his knees and crawled over to Lettie.

She was on her belly, her face turned to the left, and blood ran down her forehead and cheek. Shane leaned in close and felt the warm gust of her breath. A relieved lungful of air whooshed out of him—he hadn't realized he'd been holding it in.

"I've got to check you for broken bones. Don't get fired up at me because I'm touching you." Keeping a stream of chatter helped him focus on what he needed to do and not on the fact she was unconscious and bleeding.

He started with her head and neck, then moved his way down her shoulders and arms to her back. As he touched her body, the shape of her curves and the sweet dip at the small of her back were so familiar, he was momentarily stunned. His dreams had been real enough that he knew exactly how her hip flared out and that she had a mole on her back the size of a button.

Shane beat back the strangeness that lurked in his mind of *why* he knew. Dreams weren't real, and these sure as hell weren't memories, so how did he know her body so well?

By the time he reached her legs, he was surprised to find a sheath strapped to her thigh. Lettie carried a knife? That was one question he would ask her, even if he couldn't tell her about his dreams.

He'd pulled up her skirt to check for bruising and cuts when she startled him by speaking.

"If you pull that up any farther, I will have to stab you."

His gaze snapped to her face as joy swept through him. Her eyes were barely open to slits.

"Lettie. Jesus, I thought you were still out." He gently moved the hair back out of her face. "How do you feel?"

"Like a wagon landed on me. How do you think I feel?" She groaned and tried to push herself up.

"Easy. I haven't checked your legs yet. I need to see if anything is broken. Please." He didn't want her to make it worse by moving too soon. Field dressings could be applied using whatever he could find. Being in the war had taught him how to render first aid, amongst other things.

She sighed, sending a puff of dust in front of her face, which then made her cough. "Fine but make it fast. I'm tired of eating dirt."

He spotted a canteen lying nearby and snagged it. He would need water to clean the wounds and was glad to find he wouldn't have to go looking for it. Shane moved back to her legs and slowly lifted her skirt. She wore stockings and drawers, which were ripped and bloody. He would either need to cut them open to see the damage or take them off. Either way, Lettie was not going to be happy.

"I need to get your drawers off to tend to the wounds. Do you want me to cut them or take them off?"

There were a few beats of silence before she answered. "If I wasn't in so much pain, I would likely slap you for asking me that question. Try to cut them at the seam that way I can sew them back up and keep my dignity."

He wouldn't expect any less from her, and although the situation was far from comical, it did make his mouth kick up in a small grin. "Can I use your knife?"

She snorted. "Did you make this trip without a weapon?"

"I don't have anything, Lettie. Hell, I don't even have a pair of drawers that I own." Sadly, he didn't own the clothes on his back. The only thing he owned was his misery and his bad habits.

"Oh, that's true. Sorry. I just... Damn, yes, use the knife." Her voice told him the pain was getting worse with each passing moment.

As he took the knife from its sheath, he was glad to find it sharpened and well taken care of. She was prepared for whatever or whoever threatened her. He started to cut the delicate stitching on the plain cotton drawers when a noise drew his attention. He'd nearly forgotten about the horses. Twenty feet away, the gelding with the broken leg whinnied feebly, waiting for relief from his agony.

"Is that one of the horses?"

He grimaced. "Yes, one of them snapped his foreleg. I need to take care of him after I take care of you."

Touching her was both a pleasure and a torture. She was as soft yet firmly muscled as he imagined. He ran his hands down her lower leg first, checking for breaks, then started on the other. By the time he reached her knee, she spoke again. This time her voice was softer, thick with emotion.

"He's in pain."

"So are you. And you are more important to me than him." Well he hadn't meant to let that little bit of information slip out.

"I'm important to you?" She sounded full of surprise.

"You are my dark angel, Lettie. You brought me back from the dead whether or not I deserved it. There isn't anyone in this world who cared about me, or whether I lived or died." He set the knife down and rolled up the cotton to get a look at her leg. "Right now you are the only important person to me."

"Get on with it then. My teeth are getting gritty down here." She tried to sound grumpy, but he heard the underlying current of pain in her voice.

The knife cut through the stitching quickly, and he was checking her legs in minutes. The skin was abraded and peeled back in several places where the wagon had dragged across her legs. Dark, ugly bruises had already formed. He carefully finished checking her legs for breaks. Thank God there were none since they had no supplies and were nowhere near a doctor. He had to find a way to bandage the wounds.

He pulled off his shirt and tore off the sleeve. Someday he would pay the Gundersons back for their generosity.

Blood welled in the wounds, but not at an alarming rate. He could use the sleeve as a bandage without worrying it would soak through.

"No breaks, but there is bleeding and nasty bruises. I think you're going to be in pain for a while, but I can stop the bleeding. I'm going to clean and bandage the right leg now." He poured water on the wounds and dabbed at the skin, cleaning out the dirt and pebbles that had been ground in.

She hissed in a breath. "Shit that hurts."

Unsurprised to hear her cuss, he continued on his task. "Sorry, I'll try to be quick." He cleaned it as best he could, enduring each little noise she made as he worked. After ripping the other sleeve from the shirt, he placed one hand beneath her knee and lifted it up enough to slide the cloth beneath.

He positioned the sleeve to cover most of the wound and tied it tight enough to stay put but not too tight as to make the pain worse. Sweat stung his eyes, but he blinked it away.

God must've been watching out for this woman. The wagon should have crushed her legs. He had no explanation as to why she suffered only bruising and cuts.

The horse's cries echoed around them, cutting through Shane as he worked on Lettie. He had to stay focused, had to make sure his woman was taken care of.

His woman.

Was Lettie his? Would she ever be his? Unlikely, but it made him feel better to think of her as his woman while he worked. She was too strong to be anyone's woman, truth be told. Lettie was unique amongst women, tough as steel on the outside and prickly as hell. Inside, well, he only dreamed of how soft she was inside. Perhaps it was true. At least he could keep that illusion in his dreams.

He forced himself to work faster. The wounds on the left leg weren't as bad as they were on the right. He used the sleeve to clean her then cut off a strip from the remaining shirt to bandage her with. She sighed when he pulled the cotton back over her legs and positioned her skirt more modestly. He wouldn't tell her how much he admired her beautiful legs, the creamy skin softer than flower petals but firm from hard work. They would be perfect if they hadn't been marred by the wagon.

Now he had to make sure she was at a safe distance before he took care of the wounded gelding. The other horse kept coming over and nudging the gelding with her great nose, trying to make her partner rise. They were a matched pair, likely from the same dam, perhaps brother and sister. Same coloring and the mare was only slightly smaller than the gelding. Both of them were in distress, and he had to take care of them.

"I'm going to pick you up and set you over in the shade by those trees over there."

"Why?"

He frowned. "I need to take care of the horse, and without a gun, I'm going to have to use the knife."

"No, I won't go sit in the corner while you do the man's work. Let me help." She struggled to flip over and slapped away his hands when he tried to help. Finally she landed on her back with a grunt. "Not ideal but I can deal with the pain." She speared him with a glance, the blood drying on her cheek from cuts on her forehead. "Now give me the knife and help me over to the horse."

Shane should have argued with her, told her it was not a

woman's place to be there for blood and death. He didn't. As she was different from most women in her view of life, she was different in her view of death. She was stronger than anyone he'd ever met. He'd bet his life on that. He tucked the knife into the sheath in her thigh since he couldn't carry it and her at the same time.

"This is going to hurt." He positioned his arm beneath hers and his other arm under her knees. The worst of the injuries were to her thighs, but it was going to be painful just the same.

Slowly he lifted her, his back and knees throbbing from his own injuries. She sucked in a breath but otherwise did not complain. He got to his feet and managed not to fall on his head, but he did let out a groan.

"Am I that heavy?" Her voice was strained.

"No, but I got thrown out of the wagon too." He left it at that, not explaining that his own injuries were paltry compared to hers.

They made their way to the wounded horse. His eyes were rolling in their sockets, full of confusion and agony.

"Set me down by his head."

Shane did as she bade, positioning her so she could reach the horse. He held out his hand, and she pulled the knife from the sheath. Raw emotion showed in her expression as she put the knife in his care. He glimpsed the real Lettie behind the angry mask. She obviously felt things deeply but kept them hidden from view.

"Be as quick as you can." Her voice shook, and he didn't know if it was from physical pain or emotional.

He knelt beside the horse's head, spotting the throbbing artery at the base of his neck. It would hurt momentarily, but the horse would bleed out in minutes. Certainly wasn't as swift as a bullet to the brain but more humane than letting the horse

119

lie there and suffer.

The mare paced around them, shaking her head and whinnying a keening cry that raised goose bumps on his arms. He glanced at Lettie and nodded. She started rubbing the horse's head and speaking softly into his ear. He calmed at her crooning. Shane positioned the knife and dug in deep and quick. Blood spurted from the wound, spattering him in a hot shower of death.

Tears rolled down Lettie's face, not from her injuries, but for the struggling horse that lay dying in her arms. Shane had vowed never to cry again, but his eyes stung with unshed tears for the brave animal. The gelding struggled briefly, but as the blood flowed from the wound, he quieted. The spurts slowed along with the horse's great heart, then the blood only trickled out as death laid its cloak over the magnificent animal.

Lettie wept openly but silently. She kept petting his head after it was clear the horse had passed. The mare positioned herself behind Lettie, her nose pressed into Lettie's shoulder. The two females seemed to be helping each other through the loss.

Shane didn't hurry her, knowing Lettie grieved for the poor horse, for a life cut short because of an unforeseen accident. He knelt on the ground, covered in blood and dirt, his wounds throbbing. It was something he'd done before, in another lifetime, but now he had Lettie there. She kept the demons away with her soft strength.

He felt the earth shift beneath him as he stared at her. Lettie was more than the woman who had dragged him from the maw of death and whiskey. Much more. When Violet had died, he never expected to feel anything again, much less love. His heart had been dead long before his wife had joined it.

Lettie had resurrected it, and now it beat within his chest

once more.

The smell of blood made her sick, but she needed to sit there a little longer. The horse's life had ebbed out from him as she held his head, telling him it was okay to let go, that the pain would cease. Grief welled up within her for the horse, the unfairness of losing his life. He had been a victim, and she felt better knowing she had helped him pass.

The mare's hot breath never left her back. She seemed to need to feel Lettie's life force as her partner lay dying in the empty meadow. It comforted Lettie likely as much as it comforted the horse.

She looked up at Shane. He had been magnificent, quick and smart, getting them all through the aftermath of the wagon accident. Blood coated his bare chest and arms, his face was scraped, his hair was sticking out every which way, full of dirt and pebbles. His trousers were ripped and stained as well. He breathed heavy and gripped the knife hard enough to make his knuckles white.

"You fought in the war."

It wasn't a question. She knew by his age and by the way he acted that he'd been in battle before, knew what to do and how to assess the situation.

"Thank you for this." She scrubbed the tears from her cheeks. Her legs throbbed mercilessly along with her head. "I think I'd like to sit in the shade now."

He put the knife on the ground and crawled over to her. After nudging the mare out of the way, he picked her up and walked to the trees nearby. He set her down against the trunk of a large cottonwood tree on a bed of thick green grass.

"Are you comfortable?" His scowl should have scared her, since he looked as though he'd been in a battle. It didn't. She had never been more comfortable with a man before, and that was a miracle in and of itself.

"As much as I can be." She ran her tongue along her teeth and made a face. "Bring the canteen, will you? I've got half that meadow in my mouth."

He cupped her cheek and looked at her with so much concern, her heart did a funny flip. "I'll bring it. You're a helluva fighter, Lettie Brown."

He left her and walked toward the wreckage, his posture straight and his movements sure. If she didn't know any better, she might have believed he wasn't hurt, but he was. He'd been driving the team and had no doubt been thrown quite a distance when it wrecked.

She closed her eyes for a moment to rest. The soft breeze caressed her face, and the sound of the leaves shifting above her soothed her aches. Beside her the mare stood guard, quietly munching on the succulent grass. A peace stole over Lettie, and she let herself drift away from the pain and the horror of what the horse went through.

When she opened her eyes again, she was disoriented. She must have fallen asleep, and the late morning had given way to early afternoon.

Shane sat nearby, his legs crossed beneath him, bent over something. The sunlight cast a glow over his now-clean chest, making it appear to shine. She hadn't really looked at his chest before, but it was nicely formed. A sprinkling of molasses-colored hair whirled around his flat, copper nipples. He had numerous scars, which she had catalogued, but seeing him shirtless sent a quiver through her that had everything to do with the man in front of her.

She was attracted to him. Again.

Lettie had fought it, truly she had, but the man was under

her skin. She hadn't thought any male would ever appeal to her, but Shane did and in an elemental way. The connection between them grew stronger with each minute they were together. The wagon accident made that bond deeper. They had survived and now they were stranded halfway between home and their destination with nothing but each other, a mare with no saddle and one knife.

If it hadn't been happening to her, she might have laughed at the absurdity of the situation. She likely couldn't walk, and there was no way she could ride the horse or Shane's shoulders. A strangled laugh popped out of her mouth, and Shane's head snapped up. His gaze locked with hers, and a skitter of awareness snapped between them.

"You're awake." He got to his feet with a grimace and walked over to her, his gait stiff.

"Have you doctored your own injuries?"

He knelt beside her. "I cleaned up as best I could, but I'm gonna have to work through the rest of it. Bumps and bruises mostly."

There were fresh scratches across his cheek, and his eye, his poor eye that had taken two weeks to lose the swelling, was black and blue again. He must have landed on his face when he was thrown.

"Can I have that drink now?"

He handed her the canteen, which she hadn't seen hanging from his shoulder. The man seemed to be prepared for anything. She took one drink, swished it around and spit out the grime. A second rinse and she'd rid herself of the grit. Then she took a swallow of the sweet, cool water.

He watched her mouth and throat. She didn't know whether to be flattered or to tell him to stop staring. After using her sleeve to wipe away the water, which wasn't particularly ladylike, she handed the canteen back to him.

"Is there fresh water nearby? That tastes too good to be from Forestville." She had to distract both of them from the humming attraction in the air. It was no good for either of them.

He gestured to his right. "There's a small creek beyond the trees. Clean water, about two feet deep, enough to get most of the dirt and, um, other things off me." He was kind enough not to mention the horse's blood. Shane was a better man than she imagined him to be.

"I want to wash up too. I know I've got enough dirt in my hair to build an anthill." She scratched at her scalp. "If I can sit on the bottom of the creek, I should be okay."

His pupils dilated and his nostrils flared. "Are you sure that's a good idea? You'd need to, ah, take your clothes off."

Now it was her turn to react. Her blood quickened at the idea of disrobing in front of him. It brought back the memories of her very vivid, very erotic dreams. Ones she could not forget if she tried. There had been so much pleasure and closeness between them in those imaginings. She held them dear, never intending to tell a soul of them, particularly the man who featured in them.

"I'm sure I don't have anything you haven't seen before. Besides, after I wash up, maybe we can rustle up some of the food from the wagon." Eating would be another welcome distraction.

"Ah, yes, but I haven't seen yours. That is, we haven't... Hell, I feel like a fifteen-year-old here." He rubbed his hands down his face, the whiskers rasping against his palm. "If that's what you want, I'll help you."

Oh, she wanted more than that, much to her consternation. She wanted to see him disrobe and join her in the stream, help her wash. Was she brave enough to ask him?

124

Was it really what she wanted?

Yes and yes.

"That's what I want." She held up her arms, her heart thumping madly as he lifted her into his arms again.

This time she felt the heat of his skin, the tautness of his shoulder beneath her fingers. It reminded her of that day, weeks ago, when she helped him through his nightmare. Now he was healthier, his skin smoother. She resisted the urge to rub her hand down his back to feel how amazing she imagined it was.

What was wrong with her? How did she get to be such a wanton? After the life she'd led, there was no probability she'd want to be with a man. Yet she did. So much so that her body was ready before her mind caught up. Shane wasn't threatening. He would never hurt her. Hell, he had saved her life, doctored her wounds and cared for her as she slept. He was a good man; she knew that in her bones.

Lettie trusted her instincts, and they were screaming at her to take a chance with Shane. She had decided she couldn't be with him for good, but perhaps she could be with him for now. Use this time to erase the marks left behind by the monster who used her for his sadistic needs. It wasn't as though Shane wouldn't enjoy himself, but she would be using him for her own purposes.

She pushed aside the guilt and focused on the man. He was alive, holding her, giving her every bit of his attention. She would be a fool not to take what was right in front of her. There would likely never be another chance or another man like Shane.

They arrived at the stream in minutes, and she was pleased to see it was a private spot with plenty of shade. The fading light lent a pinkish glow to the water. He set her on the bank and looked at her clothes. It was secretly entertaining to see him struggle with what to do. She had to put him out of his misery.

"Start with my shoes while I work on my buttons."

Her legs still throbbed, but she pushed away the pain. Right now she wanted to concentrate on feeling good, feeling alive, not the remnants of a wreck that shouldn't have happened. Her fingers were stiff, but she got all the buttons undone down the front of her dress. Concentration painted his face as he worked at the knots in her laces.

"I didn't do that." She shrugged out of her sleeves. "My laces weren't all tangled like that when we left."

"It's my fault. I was trying to pull you clear from the wagon and—" He glanced up, and his gaze immediately fell to her breasts and the thin cotton chemise covering them.

Lettie didn't wear a corset. They were uncomfortable and expensive. She only wore a chemise and drawers beneath her dress. She didn't need anything else. To her surprise, her nipples had peaked and were currently poking at the material that rubbed against them.

"Ah, I had to yank a bit on the laces to get your feet out of the way." He swallowed hard enough that she heard it.

"Oh, then I reckon I owe you thanks. I didn't know, well, I guess you must've pulled me out from under the wagon." They could discuss his heroics later. Now she needed his body and his hands. "Let's get to finishing this up so I can get in that cool water. I expect it will help with the swelling and pain in my legs."

He jumped as though she'd poked him with a stick. "Sorry." He attacked the laces, his fingers pinching and pulling until he got them undone. With a sigh of relief, he tugged off one boot then the other.

"Is it okay if I, uh, take off your stockings and such?"

"A'course it is. I asked you to help, didn't I?" Lettie didn't want either one of them to feel awkward. She wanted to feel good. Now.

She lifted her hips and slid the dress past her knees. He rolled the stockings down then removed her dress. Like a lady's maid, he laid the clothing both on a nearby rock, though they were dirty and covered with rips and tears. If she wasn't so desperate to kiss him, she might have laughed at the absurdity of it.

"I ain't taking off anything else, so let's get in the water." She held up her arms again.

He shucked his trousers and boots, then shuffled back toward her sideways. She was about to ask him what the heck he was doing when she spotted the very hard cock in his borrowed drawers.

Oh my.

Her boots did that? Or rather her feet? Perhaps her breasts? Whatever body part it was, she had caused Shane Murphy to have an erection again. It pleased her to know she could have that kind of effect on him. She was, after all, not beautiful or particularly smart. Ordinary was a better description. Today, right this minute, she felt extraordinary.

He lifted her gently and made his way down into the creek. As his feet hit the water, he hissed in a breath.

"It's a little cold. Likely a mountain runoff or the like." He looked into her eyes, his gaze as hopeful as hers—probably was. "Ready?"

"Yes, I'm ready."

He lowered himself with her in his arms until he sat on the bottom of the stream.

The cold water hit her feet then her ass. She almost screamed at the frigid temperature. *A little cold?* It was more like snow in January. However the cool water lapped against her legs, then encompassed them. The sore and bruised flesh sighed in relief. It felt good, really good.

She didn't realize she'd moaned aloud until she heard it echo. She opened her eyes and peeked at him. He stared at her, not straying any lower than her chin. The man had iron control that was for sure because her nipples were so hard they ached. And they were nearly in his face.

"This feels real good, Shane." Her voice was breathy, so unlike the Lettie of the everyday variety.

"Mmm, I'm glad to hear it. The, uh, cold should be good for swelling."

The absurdity of his statement, coupled by the still-hard dick pressed against her hip, made her laugh.

His eyes widened. "What's so funny?"

"You. Me. Everything." She moved toward him until their lips were a hairsbreadth away from each other. The heated puff of his breath caressed her face, and she smiled. "Kiss me, Shane."

"I don't think that's a—"

"Now."

He focused on her mouth then licked his lips before he leaned in. She closed her eyes and waited, anticipation making her heart thump. When he finally kissed her, he was warm, so very warm and soft. She let her mouth open beneath his. At first his movements were awkward and clumsy, as though he'd forgotten how to kiss.

As their kiss deepened, he seemed to relax and remember how enjoyable it was. His tongue traced the seam of her lips, lapping one way and back again. She loved it. When his mouth settled over hers, their tongues came together as one, dancing and rasping against each other. The movements were as old as the act they mimicked.

One long, slow kiss after another, so many she lost count and lost track. She pulled back and opened her eyes, surprised to find the midday sunlight poking through the leaves in the small forest. A flock of sparrows flew past, the gentle swish of their wings echoing softly around them.

Her lips felt swollen with kisses, and they throbbed in tune with her pulse. As they stared at each other, he brushed her hair from her forehead. A simple gesture, but one that felt achingly familiar as though he'd done it a thousand times.

"Was that enough kissing?"

She shook her head. "No, now I want more than that. I want you to join with me."

His expression didn't change, but she saw a muscle jump in his jaw. "I can't."

"Oh yes you can. Don't think I don't feel that cock between us. I could count your heartbeats with it."

He frowned at her. "Kissing makes a man hard, Lettie. It don't mean nothing."

"Yes it does. It means you want to join with me." She pushed away from him, bobbing in the water enough to spread her legs. The split drawers floated in the stream like waving banners as she straddled his hips. Their combined body heat penetrated through the cold water.

"I can't do that to you, Lettie. You should only lie with your hus—"

She slapped her hand across his mouth. "Don't you dare finish that sentence. I ain't a young girl who never had a man between her legs. One day I might tell you about it. Know that I don't do this, I ain't done this, with no one in a very long time." Lettie swallowed the lump of emotion in her throat. "I want to join with you."

She had trouble putting what she felt into words, to tell him that he was special to her, that this was not an ordinary frolic in the woods. Speaking had never been something she did very well. She was the kind of person who did what she had to and showed what she meant.

So she did.

Lettie reached between them and wrapped her hand around his length. He was big, bigger than she expected, but oh so hard and hot to the touch. Shane groaned and feebly tried to pull from her grasp, but she knew if he really wanted to, he could break her hold.

She led him to the slit in her drawers, to the aching part of her that needed him inside. He held her hips and guided her forward. Together they moved until he was at her entrance.

"Lettie, I—"

"Shush now. Ain't the time to talk." With a wiggle of her hips, he was within her.

He pushed in slowly, giving her time to get used to him, which was appreciated. By the time he was fully sheathed within her, she had almost bit a hole in her lip. It was the most amazing thing she'd ever experienced. A connection with someone physically and emotionally. Her heart felt a thousand times lighter, near to bursting from her chest.

Then he started to move and it got better. His thrusts were slow and measured, enough to keep her wanting more. Her impatience grew until she couldn't take the pace any longer. She started pushing back at him as he pushed into her. Using his shoulders for leverage, she increased her speed until the water splashed between them with each plunge.

He leaned down and nudged aside her wet chemise, exposing one pink-tipped breast. She was about to ask him what he was doing when he captured it with his mouth. Pleasure zinged through her straight to her pussy. He sucked at her nipple, rolling it around on his tongue, then nibbled at it.

"Keep doing that. It feels mighty good."

Shane made a choking sound, but he didn't let that tit go. She was glad because it heightened her desire, made her push against him harder. There was something happening inside her, a tension that grew sharper and sharper. She pulled at his arms, not knowing what to do, not understanding.

Each suck of his mouth, each thrust of his cock, made the coil inside her tighten. *More. More. More.*

Lettie exploded in a whirl of colors and stars. She threw back her head and howled as the most exquisite pleasure she'd ever experienced consumed her. Her body shook with spasms, and she knew nothing more than the man in her arms and the ecstasy their joining had brought her.

He called her name and thrust deep, deep within her, his own body shuddering. Lettie felt warm tears on her cheeks, and she was glad of the water splashing at her that hid them. She'd never known what a man and woman could share.

She'd *never* known.

His chest heaved as he caught his breath, almost in unison with her gasps. It had been incredible, more than she had ever dreamed.

"I'm sorry. It's been so long, I didn't know I would lose control so fast."

He was apologizing?

"Ain't a thing to be sorry for, Shane. It felt real good." That was an understatement, but it was the best her befuddled brain could do.

"I lost control."

"Me too." If she wasn't careful, she might ask him to do it again. Hell, she'd already forgotten about the pain in her legs. There was so much of her feeling good, she didn't care about her injuries at all.

"Next time I'll make it better. I want to kiss you all over, especially the mole on your back and the birthmark on your shoulder." He grinned.

She stared at him, her breath caught somewhere between shock and scared witless. "What did you say?"

"Next time. I know maybe this is the only time but—"

"No, not that part." She pushed at his shoulders until she drifted backwards. His still-hard cock left her warm pussy, and she nearly wept from the loss. However she couldn't focus on that.

She had to focus on what he'd *said*.

"How do you know about the mole? And the birthmark?" Her heart jammed into her throat. Now she truly was frightened. "I don't understand."

His face fell as he realized what he'd said. Shane's gaze skittered away, and she knew he was trying to think of a lie. Lettie had given herself to a man, and he had likely been peeping at her, watching her undress. She felt unclean and dirty, a far cry from the satisfied woman from two minutes earlier.

"Don't ever touch me again." She managed to get to the edge of the stream and crawl out, her legs protesting each movement she made.

"Lettie, please wait."

"No, I ain't waiting. You're lucky the knife got left on the bank or I might have cut out your heart for that." Her voice was raw, full of anger and pain, a living breathing thing. "You ain't nothing to me."

"I know it doesn't make sense, but I can explain."

She heard him scramble out of the water and knew he was right behind her. Lettie tried to get to the knife lying on the rock beside her skirt, but her legs wouldn't cooperate. He dropped beside her and reached for her face. She slapped at his hands, unwilling to let him touch her, but he was too strong.

He leaned down until their faces were inches apart. She wanted to bite him, hit him and kick him until he let her go, but she couldn't do anything but hold up her body with shaking arms.

"I dreamed of you. I dreamed of touching you, pleasuring you, tasting you and being with you." His voice was jagged. "I fell in love with you in my dreams."

Lettie's heart skipped a beat. "Dreams?"

Chapter Six

Shane wanted to snatch the words back out of the air and cram them down his throat. Lettie stared at him as if she'd skin him alive then burn his dead body. Dreams! What a fool to think she would believe him. If he were a woman, he would think someone had been peeping too. There was no chance he should know about moles or birthmarks. No chance. Exactly what their future held—no chance.

His damn legs shook from the sex they'd had in the stream. In the stream, for God's sake. He'd never have thought of it, but damn it was by far the most erotic, satisfying sex he'd ever had. Now it would never be repeated thanks to his big mouth and foolish dreams.

She stared at him, her hair hanging down like a dark veil around her pale face. The wet cotton material of her underclothes clung to her, outlining her breasts, her stomach, her pussy. Unbelievably his damn dick jumped at the sight. She got off her knees, the wet sleeves still tied to her wounds, and sat on her behind.

"What dreams?" Her voice was even, but with an undertone of something else he couldn't identify. He hadn't heard it from her before.

Shane scrambled for something to say that didn't sound as dumb as he felt. In the end he decided being honest was the only option. What the hell? It certainly couldn't get any worse.

"I've had dreams about us, me and you together. It started a few days after I got here. Each dream gets clearer, and I see things like the room, the lantern, even your hairbrush on the chest of drawers." He tried not to get caught up in exactly how arousing the dreams had been and focused on the facts. "We, uh, pleasure each other in different ways. Almost like we're married or something."

That part always bothered him. He'd been married once, and he'd lost her because of his own failings as a man. The dreams were only conjurings of his imagination. He would never marry again and risk losing a woman he loved. It wasn't in the cards.

She stared at him in silence without flinching. He finally decided enough was enough and got to his feet. Lettie could think what she wanted. He'd been truthful, and there wasn't anything else he could say.

He glanced down and noted his drawers were as see-through as her chemise, but it wasn't as though she hadn't seen him naked before. Hell the woman had undressed him before they had a *how-do-you-do*. He walked toward his clothes, which were lying beside her dress, when she whispered something.

Shane turned to look at her. He couldn't possibly have heard her right.

"What did you say?"

She glanced down at her hands, her face hidden. "I had dreams too."

His stomach flipped once then again. He dropped to the grass beside her, his trousers clutched in his hands.

"That can't be."

"I know it can't, but it is." She shook her head. "You have a strawberry birthmark at the back of your hair, hidden beneath the curls. You're ticklish on the bottom of your feet, and you love it when I tease you by undressing real slow."

Shane couldn't find one word to say. He felt like he'd been punched in the head. A thirst for a shot of whiskey roared through him. God he needed a drink in the worst way.

"That's not possible. We can't have had the same dreams."

"I reckon it is possible because it happened." She finally turned to look at him, her eyes wide. "I don't know what it means, but it scares me deep down, enough to make my bones rattle. We're strangers, Shane. We barely know each other. But I know how much you like your earlobes nibbled."

He sucked in a breath as his blood pounded through his head. Just not possible.

"The last dream you had, where were we? What did it look like?"

"In my bedroom at the house. Small with one window facing south. There were candles on the chest of drawers and on the table in the corner." She recited the scene, and it came back to him in a rush. "I was wearing a new nightdress, and it was silky soft."

"Holy shit. Holy shit. *Holy shit.*" He wondered if he were dreaming right then, but the breeze on his wet skin told him different. "What else?"

She shook her head. "It was the first time I rode you."

Shane shot to his feet and left her sitting there as he walked out into the meadow toward the wreckage of the wagon. He could hardly catch his breath, and his thoughts were jumping like frogs in his head. Leaving Lettie by the stream was cruel considering she couldn't really walk. But right about then, he would go completely loco if he didn't get a moment away from her.

He sank to his knees, shaking and gulping in air. He didn't understand what was going on. Somehow they'd had the same dreams, down to the last detail. The dream of her climbing on

136

him, putting his cock inside her, was vivid enough to be a memory.

But it never happened.

Shane sat there for a while until his body and his drawers dried. He pulled his trousers back on and fastened the suspenders. His shoes were back at the stream along with his dream lover, the woman who had already turned his life inside out and upside down. Now he had to figure out how to sort out the real from the imagined without hitting the bottle in the process.

He stood and walked toward the wagon, the soft meadow tickling his feet. She'd been completely right about him, everything was correct. His feet were ticklish.

Shane circled the wagon, giving the horse's body a wide berth. He gathered up the supplies and materials he could use. It gave his hands something to do and kept his thoughts at bay. He found a blanket underneath the wagon along with the basket that used to hold the food from the restaurant. Earlier he'd salvaged the edible food for them. The basket might be repaired by someone who was handy with them.

When he walked back to the tree line holding the blanket and basket, he was more in control. The crazy notion that they had shared dreams, erotic realistic ones, was something he would have to accept. No matter that it didn't make sense or that no one would believe them. He'd accepted the strange link between them. What they'd do next was as unknown as how they would get home.

Home.

He must have started thinking of Forestville and the Blue Plate as home. If he'd been asked a month ago, Shane would have said he had no home and no plans for one. Now he thought about how worried Marta would be and how fussy

Pieter would be since the wagon was not going to make it back today. It would never be back unless they found a way to repair the smashed end and pulled it back to the livery they'd borrowed it from. Shane hoped the Gundersons did not have to pay for the wagon. The wheel had shattered in mid-motion. If anyone was to blame, it was the owner of the livery for renting a wagon that so obviously needed to be taken care of.

Shane was thinking about what he'd say to the man when the hairs on the back of his neck stood at attention. He dropped into a crouch and looked around, but nothing was amiss. Lettie was still down at the stream. Perhaps the danger he sensed was related to her. He left the blanket and basket and crashed through the woods as fast as he could.

He skidded to a stop, sliding the last few feet on the wet grass. Three men surrounded Lettie, a ragtag group who didn't have a clean spot anywhere on their faces or clothes. Memories slammed into him, stealing his ability to think for a moment. God wouldn't be so cruel as to give him another woman to lose like this. He shook off the dark thoughts with more strength than he thought he had. Now wasn't the time to get lost in his own stupid mistakes. Lettie was the important one right now. He let anger replace the stark, cold panic.

Shane growled at them as he got to his feet. He wished he had a gun or any other weapon to protect her. Her knife was gone from the rock, and he hoped like hell she'd been able to grab it before the men showed up. They needed something to use or they risked more than their lives from these three.

"Who's this fella, Lettie?" The big one eyeballed him with a cold stare. The fact he knew Lettie's name sent a chill down Shane's spine.

This is not Missouri. She is not Violet and you are not drunk. Steady, Shane, steady.

"My intended, Shane Murphy. I told you he was coming back." Her hair was still wet, but she'd at least pulled on her dress. If she'd been just wearing her underclothes, the men might have done worse than threaten her.

It hit him that she'd called him her intended as though they were going to be hitched. He tried not to think about that since there wasn't much of a chance of it happening. Hell, they'd be lucky to get back to Forestville or survive the men currently looming over them. He never thought he'd actually be glad not to have whiskey in his veins. His thinking was clearer, and damned if he wasn't ready to start throwing punches.

"What do you want?" Shane snapped. "We don't have anything."

"Oh I wouldn't say that." The big one's gaze slid to Lettie.

Shane growled again, a feral sound from deep inside his gut.

"I don't think he likes you, Buster." The skinny one on the right laughed like a loon. "You'd best be careful." Another guffaw.

"He ain't got nothin', remember?" The big one, obviously named Buster, was smarter than the rest. He appeared to be sharp and keen, unlike his cohorts. "Besides, he ain't gonna do a thing against three of us."

Shane glanced at Lettie. Instead of being afraid, she appeared to be furious. If she'd had a gun, no doubt she would have shot all of them. He was proud of her. The woman had a backbone worthy of any soldier. She wouldn't fall to pieces and offer her child to save herself. Shane beat back the memories creeping in on him again.

Focus.

"Be on your way then." Slowly, Shane sidled closer to Lettie, his instincts screaming and on edge. The men were

139

seeing how far they could go.

"Oh no, I don't think so. You see, I know Miss Lettie has money from the folks in town. A lot of money." Buster's grin was as hideous as it was disturbing. "I want that money."

Shane had no inkling that Lettie was carrying a great sum of money. It should have occurred to him that she would have to have funds to pay for the supplies, but the Gundersons could have wired the money too. If she were carrying money, they were in danger. Plenty of it.

"I don't know what you're talking about, Buster. Pieter wouldn't trust money with me or anyone. He's too stingy." Lettie reached her hand up, and Shane grasped it, pulling her to her feet. She wobbled a bit, but she stood straight and tall next to him.

Her willingness to stand on her painful, bruised legs gave him courage and confidence. He put his arm around her waist and anchored her to him. No reason the men should know she was vulnerable and wounded.

"That's not what I heard from Alice." Buster *tsk*ed at her. "That little honey girl told me all about your trip and how folks are counting on those supplies."

Alice must be the type who enjoyed sharing secrets, which surprised him because she never spoke to Shane when she brought him food. The girl didn't seem to be the kind to stir the pot, but perhaps she liked to gossip. It didn't matter any which way because she had gotten them into a situation they had to get out of, fast.

"Alice is a pain in the ass," Lettie snapped. "She does nothing but brag to get men to fall in love with her or at least into her drawers."

"She didn't let me in her drawers." Buster's smile faded. "I got what I needed anyway."

The big man's leer told Shane he'd used force, had probably threatened Alice, until she revealed the information about the money Lettie carried. Damn.

"You got nothing. She lied to you, Buster, like she does every time you, Norman and Myron come into the restaurant. The money is in Benson waiting for us at the bank." Lettie trembled against him. Her strength was fading, but her courage was still strong.

"Then we're going to Benson." Buster gestured to the other two men, and they both pulled out pistols, pointing them straight at Shane and Lettie. "Let's go."

Shane tightened his grip on Lettie's waist. "We are not walking to Benson. You saw that wagon. We aren't going anywhere."

"Don't you worry. We planned on either getting the money or the supplies. I got a wagon east of here." Buster gestured with his pistol. "Get to walking. Now."

Lettie made a small noise, a tiny sound of distress, but it reverberated through him like a shot. Shane hadn't experienced such white-hot fury in a long time. He wanted to kill all of them for scaring her, for making her walk when she could barely stand. There wasn't much of a choice to make. He would have to carry her.

Before she could protest, he picked her up as gently as he could and settled her against him. With her in his arms, they were vulnerable to attack, but he wasn't going to let Lettie's pride dictate the course to follow. She couldn't walk, but he could.

"What the hell are you doing, Murphy?" Buster frowned at him.

"You wanted us to walk. We're walking." The piece of shit didn't deserve an explanation, and Shane wasn't going to give him one.

"You can put me down," she whispered. "I think I can walk."

"Stay put and be quiet, Lettie. Keep your eyes open and watch them." His whisper was more like an order hissed through clenched teeth.

She didn't protest again, but she stiffened in his arms. No doubt she would let him know later exactly what she thought of his high-handedness. For now, she let him take the lead, thank God. Lettie wasn't a big woman, but he had only recently recovered from his near-death beating. Today's wagon accident should have killed him.

He was sore and weak, much as he wouldn't tell her that. She already had a low opinion of him. Sweat beaded on his forehead and back, his muscles screamed, but he refused to slow down even a little. When his breath started coming in painful bursts, he kept walking. Shane gritted his teeth, unwilling to give up or admit defeat.

It seemed like hours before the wagon came into view. He felt a poke in the back and stumbled. After he righted himself, Lettie frowned at him then turned her gaze to Buster.

"If you poke him again, I will smack the grin right off your face, Buster Dawson." Her voice held the promise she would do exactly what she threatened.

"I'm funning with your man, Lettie. He sounds like a locomotive huffin' and puffin'." Buster was likely smirking at him. The son of a bitch was enjoying himself.

"We had a wagon accident, you fool. Of course he's huffing and puffing." Lettie tightened her arm on his shoulder.

"Maybe it's your fat ass that's the problem."

This time she tried to hit the man, much to Shane's

satisfaction. "You are a jackass."

"And you are a bitch."

Fury ripped through him. Shane stopped short and wasn't surprised when Buster cursed behind him. No doubt he almost ran into him.

"If you ever call her that or any other name again, I will rip your fucking tongue out of your mouth. I don't care if you empty your pistol into me, I'll die with your goddamn tongue clenched in my fist." He looked at Lettie's shocked expression. "She is not a bitch and doesn't have a fat ass. She is a lady and deserves respect."

A few moments went by before Buster responded. "I don't mean nothin' by it. I've been joshin' with her for a year." The petulant tone in his voice meant he took Shane's threat seriously. Good. He was serious.

Shane would not disappoint his woman or let her down. This was his chance to redeem himself, at least in part, for his past sins. Even if he died trying.

They arrived at the wagon, which was a sorry-looking rig that had been misused for some time. There were jagged and missing boards, dirt and spots of God only knew what coated the bed, and the horses strapped to the front were swayback nags. A stained tarp hung off one side. It would not be a comfortable ride, that was certain.

Shane set Lettie in the bed of the wagon in the cleanest spot he could find. He took a few deep breaths and got the first whiff of the stench surrounding the rig. It made his eyes water, and he wished he hadn't chosen that spot to catch his breath.

"What is that smell?" Lettie wrinkled her nose.

"I don't smell nothin'." The skinny one looked at them as though he'd never heard such a strange question.

"Myron, you can't smell nothing anyway." Buster pushed him aside and reached into the wagon beneath the tarp. When he pulled out a handful of rope, he heard Lettie's intake of breath.

"You are not tying me up, Buster." Her voice sounded strained.

"Oh yes I am. Ain't no way I'm letting you ride back there without making sure you cain't go nowhere." Buster shook the rope at Shane. "Your man here already wants to yank out my tongue."

It was true. Shane wouldn't sit docilely in the back while they drove to Benson to rob the Gundersons. As it was, he was looking at their weapons and judging how he could possibly overwhelm all of them. If there had been only two of them, he could have had a chance, but the three of them were armed with weapons and their own stupidity.

Buster had come around with the ropes and reached for Lettie. She slapped at his hands and tried to scramble backwards, hindered by her wounded legs. Shane moved to get between them, but Myron and the silent third man took hold of his arms. Someone had shoved a pistol in his back, preventing him from elbowing them in the face.

Frustration ate away at him as he watched Lettie struggle. She scratched and punched Buster, but he was stronger than she was. Shane growled as the other man used his knee to hold her down on her stomach in the filthy wagon.

"Let her go."

"Shut up, Murphy. I could kill you both and get me what I want." Buster grunted as Lettie kicked him in the back. "She's gettin' tied up and then you are too. I ain't takin' no chances. I want that money."

That was all the men wanted. Money. It was the reason

most men killed or worse. He pulled against the arms holding him, but they were iron tight. Helpless fury swept through him, and all he saw was red.

Buster finished tying Lettie's wrists and feet. When he started to hogtie her, Shane managed to free one arm and punched Myron in the balls. Momentarily free, Shane leapt at Buster, who still held down Lettie with his knee. Shane would not allow him to hurt her any more than the son of a bitch already had.

"Stop him," Buster snarled.

Shane got one punch into the big man's face, pleased to hear a satisfying crunch of his nose. Then something hit him in the back of his head and everything went black. The last thing he saw was Lettie's stricken face, her cheeks stained with tears.

Don't cry, Lettie.

Lettie wanted to kill Buster. Not for tying her up but for trying to kill Shane. He was still alive and breathing beside her in the wagon beneath the tarp, but he was pale. There was dried blood on his hair and neck. That idiot Norman had used his rifle to knock Shane unconscious, and judging by the sick pleasure on his face, Norman had enjoyed doing it.

The smell under the tarp had become bearable only because her nose was clogged. She'd been crying, something she'd vowed never to do again. Big words for a cowardly woman. As soon as Buster had started to tie her up, memories washed over her and Lettie had panicked. She'd fought against him, but he was too strong. All she'd managed to do was make him angry and put Shane in a position that ended in another injury. He'd also taken their shoes, presumably so she and Shane couldn't run away even if they were untied.

The scratchy rope rubbed at her wrists. Buster had tied

145

them too tight on purpose as he whined that Shane had broken his nose and stained his shirt. Lettie asked him how he could tell, judging by the filth already encrusted on his damn shirt. That notched up his anger to fury, and he not only tightened the ropes until she started to lose feeling in her fingers, but he also made sure he hogtied her too tight.

Her back arched because there was barely two feet of rope between her ankles and wrists. She felt like a piece of wood bent into an unnatural circle, ready to splinter or break. Her wounded legs were screaming in agony. She shook from the pain coursing through her as though a river of anguish rolled down her back with every breath. Lettie had endured such pain before, but she had hoped it would never happen again. The key was to distract herself from her own discomfort. She had to focus on the man in front of her who'd tried valiantly to save her.

Shane might have started out their relationship by puking on her shoes, but he had since proven himself a gentleman, one who deserved better than this. Buster had tied him the same way—the vicious jerks on the ropes on an unconscious man had made her flinch. Buster was out of control, and she had no doubt their hog-tied bodies would end up in a ravine somewhere, shot through the head and left for scavengers.

She accepted that she'd found what she didn't know she was looking for—love. She'd fallen in love with Shane. Lettie hadn't recognized it for what it was until now, when their lives were at risk and time was more precious than any treasure. Shane was as broken as she was inside, a man who had endured his own private hell but survived. He was strong, brave, considerate, gentle and the only man in the world she ever wanted to be with.

She closed her eyes and thought of their lovemaking in the stream. The cool water had lapped around them as his hot mouth pleasured her breast. She'd experienced incredible joy she'd never known existed until he had opened the door to it. Lettie could still feel his hands, his wonderful hands, on her skin. When she'd first seen him, his gray eyes had appeared dead, but now she knew better. They churned with passion, their swirling depths full of life.

Until this moment, when she stared at his unconscious, bloody face, she hadn't realized how much he had come to mean to her. Or that what she was feeling was love. Now she understood Sam and Angeline and their devotion to each other. She understood the affection they showed and the private looks they shared. Finally, Lettie understood.

And now it might be too late.

She wouldn't let the impossible situation deter her from trying to find a way to beat the bastards who held them captive. Somehow they had to escape from the three men, and it wasn't going to happen while they were tied. Buster was smart but not as smart as Lettie. She was dirty, disheveled and wore the evidence of the wagon accident. How were they going to explain all that, plus the rope, to the bank in Benson?

Her one advantage was that the money wasn't in the bank. It was sewn into the waist of her skirt in pouches she had added herself a year ago. It kept the little money she had safe, and thank God she'd used it for the Gundersons' money this time. Buster was too stupid to realize she was lying.

When they arrived at the bank for money that wasn't there, she could only hope they would give up and run for the hills. The other possibility, that they would rob the bank or kill Lettie and Shane, was not what she wanted to consider. There had to be a way to get free of the ropes and sneak away before Buster and his men realized anything was wrong.

Of course at that moment she couldn't scratch her nose if

she wanted to.

Shane's rusty voice startled her. "I hope you're thinking about how to escape."

He was awake. Thank God! Relief coursed through her. She had been afraid another injury to his head would do permanent damage to his brain. She'd heard of such a thing before, and the possibility was very real.

"Of course I am. I haven't thought of any brilliant plan yet though."

"Keep trying. You're smart enough to figure it out." Shane moaned when he tried to move. "Did he make sure the knots were tight enough for me to lose feeling in my hands and feet? Jesus Christ, my head hurts. And why am I barefoot?"

She wanted to comfort him, pull him into her arms and kiss his wounds, especially the one he'd received trying to save her. His courage had been inspiring, and now she would do her best to show the same kind of courage. She had to beat back the scared Lettie and find the brave one who would do her man proud.

"They took our shoes. I guess to make sure we didn't run away. Maybe if we flipped over and our hands were close enough, we could untie each other?"

Lettie had no idea if she could move, much less turn. That was beside the point. Untying each other was still a good idea.

"That might work if I could make my hands move. I don't know if I still have all ten fingers." He made a strangled sound. "Nope, I can't feel my arms either. Fucking bastard."

"He's smart but not that smart. If we can get free, I know we can outwit him and the two fools with him."

"How do you know him?" Shane's voice held a hint of what she thought might be jealousy. How extraordinary.

"They work on a ranch near Forestville. Come in every Sunday for breakfast while other folks are in church. Buster's big, mean and ornery. Norman and Myron are just dumb cowpokes. But Buster, he likes to bully people, like Alice." She would find out exactly what Buster had done to the girl when they got back to Forestville. Whatever it was, it wasn't good.

"He's a son of a bitch who deserves to swing for what he did to you." Shane nearly snarled his threat, full of vengeance. It surprised her at the same time it made her feel better. Someone cared enough about her to seek revenge because of wrongs done to her. No one had looked out for her before Angeline. No one had protected her until Shane.

"Don't do anything you could swing for yourself."

"Stop fighting me, Lettie. I know this is hard to believe, but I used to be a soldier. I know how to wage war." His voice had lost its edge and sounded flat, disturbing to hear.

She tried to make out his face in the shadows of the tarp. "Tell me."

"Not now."

"You have something that needs doing?" Lettie snorted softly. "I don't know anything about you."

"You know I'm a drunk."

"You know I'm a bitch. Is that who you think I am?" Her voice took on an edge, and her panic began to creep in again. She needed to be distracted, and fighting with Shane would work.

"No, I think you've been hurt bad enough to punch first and talk later. I think you have a big heart that you hide behind the walls around you."

She managed not to try to bite him, but it was a near thing. "At least I'm not a drunk."

His laugh was anything but humorous. "Punch first, talk later."

"Stop it."

"No I won't. You can be a mean bitch, but I've seen you be an angel." He shifted closer. "Stop pushing me away, Lettie. A little while ago, I was inside you. I know who you are underneath all that."

"Stop it." Her voice wavered as her heart wept silently.

"Who hurt you?"

She couldn't begin to tell him. How could he like her if he knew?

"I've done a lot of things I'm not proud of, been to hell and back more than once. Believe me, there is nothing you can tell me that would be worse than my crimes." He sounded profoundly sad, as though he had been responsible for the evil done across the world.

"I don't believe that. You aren't that bad."

There was that horrible laugh again. "After the war I came home and became a drunk. Any money we had went to whiskey. I cared more about a drink than I did my wife and daughter."

Wife and daughter.

"You have a daughter?" Her heart pinched. Hard. The idea he had a child somewhere stole her breath.

"Not anymore. She's dead because of me, just like her mother." He leaned in close. "You see, I was rip-roaring drunk in the barn, passed out in the loft, when a group of ex-soldiers came to my ranch. I imagine she screamed for me for a while before I came to."

Lettie was transfixed by the sound of his voice and the agony in his story.

"What happened?"

"She was the daughter of a rich man, stuck in a dirt farmer's ranch with a child, while I fought in the war. When I got back, she tried to force my daughter to like me. The girl was too smart for that, she knew Daddy was bad news. I stayed out of their way, and they did their best to fool people into thinking I was worth a shit." He blew out a breath. "The day they died was cloudy, so the loft was darker than usual. I remember thinking I was dreaming she called me, then I realized it was her voice. When I stumbled out of the barn, I heard what she said."

Lettie leaned in close to hear. His voice had gotten softer with each word. "What did she say?"

"She offered them E-Elizabeth, her daughter, *our* daughter. She traded our child to save her own life." If words could cry, his would have been weeping. The raw emotion was potent, full of self-loathing, regret and heartache. "I remember screaming and reaching for her throat. I don't know what happened after that, but when I came to, they were both dead. I left the farm that day, told the sheriff what happened and never went back. You see, I destroyed them sure as if I had killed them myself. I didn't deserve a wife or a daughter."

"I'm sorry." It was the best she could do, although it couldn't possibly convey how she felt. His misery was akin to hers. Her tragedies were numerous and as colossal as his.

"Violet should never have married me."

Lettie's heart skipped a beat. "Who?"

"My wife, Violet Simpson. She should never have married me." He cursed softly. "I can't even bear to speak or hear their names. Burns like poison on my soul."

She contemplated telling him that her real name was Violet Elizabeth, but she couldn't. To know her name, her real name,

151

would cause him such agony was unthinkable. Another time, another place, she would tell him. The coincidence was eerie. For now, she would comfort him the best way she knew how. By telling him some of her own nightmares.

"I was born in Utah, raised in the ward. You probably don't know what that is, hmm? It's part of a religion called Latter-day Saints. Most folks go about their days and lives just fine. I was born to a weak woman and an overbearing man. She died giving birth to me, and my father sent me to live with strangers until I was five." She could picture the tiny corner she slept in at the Michaels household, a hazy image that had lost its detail. "They were good people, but when I was five, I was able do chores and my father wanted me back. I lived in terror of him, cleaning the house, burning myself while I tried to cook, doing laundry even though I couldn't reach the top of the wash bin."

"You had no one else to help?"

"No one. My father was an only child, and his parents were dead. My mother was an outsider, a woman he had brought in. It was his punishment that she died and that he had a lazy, ugly child."

"You are not lazy or ugly." Shane scoffed. "You work harder than anyone I've ever known. And you're beautiful, honey."

"Kind of you to say, but I don't know if I can ever believe it. Twenty years passed that I worked until my fingers bled and I would fall asleep exhausted in bed each night. Eventually I figured out how to do everything I needed to. No one would teach me because I was only half-LDS. The women shunned me, and the men ignored me. Other children were forbidden from playing with me. I had nothing and no one until I was twenty-five." She swallowed the huge lump in her throat at the memory of such a silly, naïve girl. "When Josiah Brown offered for me, my father refused, but I pleaded with him, endured extra beatings, until he relented. I was so shocked to be chosen by a high-ranking member of our ward that I ignored any warning signs. I reckon I didn't figure being second wife was going to be too taxing."

"Did you say second wife?"

"One of the basic covenants of LDS is that a man may have multiple wives. It works out well for the women because they share the burden of taking care of him and the children. I know of many happy marriages, but not mine." Bitter memories of her first days of marriage crowded her mind. "I didn't realize the extent of Josiah's sick ways for a week. By then it was too late and I was truly his wife."

"What did he do to you, Lettie?" The concern and love in Shane's voice gave her courage to keep going.

"For five years, I was married to a monster. He only found pleasure in hurting others or watching women pleasure each other. His first wife died, and I think it was because she wanted to escape and that was the only way. Then he wanted Angeline. He had to have two women or there was no fun, you see. And Angeline is so beautiful it makes my eyes hurt."

"She is stunning, but she's not you," Shane pronounced. "I'd rather have my dark angel than one I'm afraid I'll break."

Lettie barked a laugh. "She is stronger than anyone I ever met. That girl at eighteen endured whippings that would have broken any man. She was the first person to care about me, the only person to hug me, and my first friend. Without her I'd still be under Josiah's thumb, surviving, because that's what I know how to do."

"You left him?" Shane had moved nearer, his forehead close enough to touch hers.

"We ran from him. Traveled here, scared, without any money or idea of where we were going. When we found the Blue

Plate, we thought it was temporary. Then a hired killer showed up to seek revenge for the wrongdoing we had done to Josiah."

Shane reared back. "What?"

"It's true. He hunted us down to kill us. Angeline's sister Eliza is the only reason we're alive. She convinced him not to kill anyone, and strange as it may be, she married him. Josiah came after us himself after he knew where we were." She pressed her forehead against his. "An old beau of Angeline's, Jonathan, killed him before he had a chance to shoot her."

She let the story settle over him before she continued. "I ain't a catch, Shane. I'm damaged inside and out. I didn't know what love was, and I have fits where I can't breathe and I curl into a ball. I'm ornery, mean and I have no patience either."

This was it. The moment he could let her go or accept her for the pitiful excuse for a woman she was. Lettie wasn't ready for her heart to be broken so soon, but better now than later.

"We are a matched set. I'm damaged inside and out too. I'm going straight to hell for everything I've done and haven't done." Shane's chuckle was punctuated with a sob. "I'd say there isn't another person in the world who could be with us except each other."

Lettie knew then her heart had made the right and only choice. Something had thrown this man in her path, literally, and she had finally accepted it was meant to be. Now they had to survive their kidnapping and find a way to overcome their demons long enough to be happy.

They stayed that way, forehead to forehead, their breaths mingling as their memories and their pain had. It was a perfect moment, one that made her throat tight and her heart ache for both of them. God had put some fierce obstacles along the paths their lives had taken. Perhaps they could banish the darkness they both lived in by changing the path they were currently on.

Lettie leaned forward, took a deep breath and rolled back as far as she could, then forward until she landed on her stomach. She turned her face to the side to avoid the dirt and splinters.

Shane eyed her with a frown. "What are you doing?"

"Flipping over so I can untie you. Weren't you paying attention to me?"

His frown deepened. "I don't think this is a good idea. I can't feel my hands. Weren't you paying attention to me?"

Lettie found herself smiling at his retort. He was annoyed that she was trying to get them free when he couldn't. After their sharing of souls, a little arguing would be just the thing to chase the dark memories away.

"That's why I'm going to do the untying." She rolled again until she was on her right side. "Now you flip over and I'll get to work."

He sighed hard enough to make dirt move past her ear. "I don't think this will—"

"Stop yapping and start doing. I don't know how long we'll have."

Several moments went by before she heard him shift. A few grunts and curses and thumps later, his hands grazed hers.

"I still can't feel my hands. Am I in the right spot?"

"Yep and I can feel your fingers." She closed her eyes and focused on his hands. She had to move a little nearer, then down a bit. His fingers felt swollen and cold. It bothered her that Buster had tied his hands tight enough to cause permanent damage. She promised herself to make Buster pay for that particular sin.

Lettie picked at the knots as best she could, but it was slow and painful. The rope was rough but cheap, the only advantage she had. The strands started to unravel as she worked at it. Her fingers grew slippery, and she hoped it was sweat and not blood.

She had no idea how much time had passed before she felt the first knot give. With a triumphant but silent hoot, she got to work on the next one. Her hand started to cramp, but she didn't stop or slow down. Lettie gritted her teeth, keeping her eyes closed so the dirt and sweat wouldn't make them sting.

When the last knot gave way, she almost wept with relief. Shane groaned and shifted beside her. Soon she felt him fumbling with the knots on her hands.

"Sorry if I'm slow. I'm getting the feeling back and it hurts like hell. Feels like a million knives stabbing my hands. Dammit." He paused, and she heard his hands rubbing together, skin on skin. "I'm sorry, honey."

Honey.

This time the word felt natural, and she accepted it for what it was—a true sign of his affection for her. At least she hoped he had affection for her. It would be horrible if she had fallen in love with him and he didn't feel the same way. Now was not the right place to be thinking about affection and love, but she couldn't stop herself. Her emotions were running high, and since she'd let them loose, she wasn't going to be able to control them.

"Do you like me, Shane?"

He started on the knots on her hands again. "What?"

"Do you like me?"

"You are a pain in the ass, you're bossy and you are mean. How could I not like you?" He sounded as though he was talking through gritted teeth.

"I can't tell if you're funning me or if you mean it." His response bothered her, more than she wanted him to know. It was important that she knew how he felt, not simply wondered. There hadn't been anyone like him in her life, and there wouldn't ever be another.

He leaned forward until his mouth was beside her ear. "I can't exactly declare my love for you in the back of a dirty wagon while you're hog-tied like the letter C. If you give me a little while to save our lives, I can be a better poet."

Her heart leapt into her throat. "Does that mean you love me?"

"Jesus Christ, Lettie, I can't believe you're—"

"Answer the question, Murphy. Now." There was no chance she could ride the rest of the way to Benson without knowing the truth.

"Yes, I love you. Now shut up and let me do what I need to do."

Lettie hugged his words to her heart and blinked away the sting of tears, this time happy ones. It wasn't a profession of undying devotion she might have wanted, but it was what fit. Their relationship was not normal, and neither should their love be.

"Good, because I do too."

He paused again, although she could feel the ropes were beginning to loosen around her wrists. "You do what?"

Lettie could hardly form the words, the very thing she had forced him into admitting.

"Don't you dare pretend you don't know what I'm talking about." He nibbled on her earlobe. "Tell me."

Lettie squeezed her eyes shut. "OkayIloveyou." It came out in a rush, a single word that made up the sum of all the whirling emotions in her heart and in her gut.

His chuckle puffed across her cheek. "If we live after today, I think I might have to hear you say that again."

A bubble of happiness expanded inside her, a warm, comfortable presence. She was more than content, she was happy. For the first time in her life, she finally understood what happy felt like. She wanted it to last forever, to hold it close like the treasure it was. But Lettie would take what she had, which was here and now.

Her hands were suddenly loose, and blood rushed through her fingers. The tingles turned into pins, and she sucked in a pained breath. Her knots hadn't been as tight as Shane's, and she could only imagine how much his hands hurt. Yet he hadn't stopped. He worked at her knots until he got them untied. How could she have ever felt he was a worthless drunk?

"Thank you."

"Let's get our feet untied. Don't sit up because they'll see the tarp move. We have to let them believe we're still tied up under here." Shane slid backwards and pulled his feet up.

Lettie did the same, her hands complaining loudly as she picked at the rough hemp again. It didn't surprise her that Buster had cheap rope. He was cheap from top to bottom. Within a few minutes her ankles were free, and she breathed a sigh of relief. Whatever happened, she would at least be able to face her fate standing on her own feet.

"I'm going to shimmy down to the end of the wagon and see what I can see." Shane shifted beside her.

"So am I."

"Oh no you're not. Stay here. What if one of those fools takes a shot at us? I sure as hell am not going to be responsible for you getting a new hole in your head." Shane was getting bossy, and she didn't like it one bit.

"And you need a hole in your head?" she snapped.

"No, but I'm the man. It's my job to protect you, so let me."

She heard his body scrape down the bed of the wagon to the end. Lettie waited about five seconds before she followed him.

"Go back to where you were, woman."

"Make me."

He sighed so hard, she swore the tarp moved. "You are a pigheaded mule."

"And you're a stubborn jackass. Now shut up and let's get to seeing what we can see." She wanted to have the advantage over Buster and his men, however little it was.

Shane looked out the left side while she looked out the right. "Don't move it more than an inch or so."

"I can figure that out by myself."

He mumbled a curse but didn't tell her to move again. Lettie understood the need to protect, but she had to make him understand she was not a wilting flower of femininity. The only thing feminine she could attest to were her body parts. Everything else was as it was—she did what needed doing.

She peered through the tarp. Norman rode directly behind the wagon. He was busy scratching his balls, which didn't surprise her, but he blocked their escape. She couldn't see Myron or Buster but assumed one of them drove the ragtag wagon.

"We've got a rider back here. It's the skinny, stupid one," Shane whispered.

"Myron." Lettie made a face. "Norman's riding on this side. Neither one of them is very smart, but you don't need that to fire a gun."

"We're not going to slip out the back and escape, that's for sure." He turned to look at her. "We can surprise them when the wagon stops, but that's dangerous."

"And what part of this adventure isn't dangerous?" She scooted closer to him. "There are three of them. Even the strongest man would have trouble taking on three-to-one odds. I've got tits, but I've also got a knife and a whole lot of anger. I can be fierce."

"You already are fierce." He moved closer still until they were nose to nose again.

She wouldn't tell him, but she enjoyed their banter quite a bit. More than she probably should considering they were arguing and insulting each other. Another interesting aspect of their unconventional relationship.

"Don't forget it."

"As if I could forget it. Woman, you are asking to go to war."

"We're at war. Buster and those two morons threatened us, beat you, tied us up and are forcing us to take money from the very people who saved us." Lettie narrowed her eyes, her heartbeat steady and sure. "I ain't opposed to killing them if it comes to it."

His gray gaze studied her as he appeared to be mulling over her words. "You would have been a good soldier. Better than me."

"They don't let you soldier if you have tits."

Shane stifled a snort by slapping his hand over his mouth. The raw skin of his wrist gleamed in the meager light under the tarp. He might consider himself a poor soldier, but she knew better. The man had lived through a great deal, and he was still a good man, one who had honor and courage. She wouldn't let him put himself down, especially when she knew the truth of the matter.

"We're going to have to fight for our lives."

Lettie nodded. "Then let's give them a fight."

He kissed her hard. "You're a helluva woman."

She grinned at him, ready to fight to keep the incredible gift she'd been given—a man who loved her and accepted her for who she was. It was a gift worth fighting for.

Chapter Seven

Shane was in pain, but he wouldn't tell Lettie how much. His hands felt like a horse had stomped on them. Buster had decided to cause a little extra discomfort when he tied Shane up. Lousy bastard deserved a taste of his own medicine. If Shane had the chance, he would return the favor in kind.

The wagon lumbered along toward Benson, and he assumed they were close. He had no idea how much time had passed since he'd been unconscious, but it couldn't have been that long. He and Lettie had been huddling under the tarp for at least an hour waiting for their chance to take control back from the three men who held them captive.

She was incredible, braver than any man he'd ever known. After she told her story of her life, her marriage and her escape, he'd been in awe of how much courage she had. Now she was ready to take on three men with a single knife. Damn good thing Buster hadn't checked her for weapons. He would have lost some fingers, of that Shane was certain.

He didn't know how long they had before the wagon stopped, but they had to be on guard. Their only advantage was surprise. He looked over at Lettie and saw the knife clutched in her hand. She stared at the side of the tarp, her expression fiercer than the blade.

"Can you use that thing?"

She scowled at him. "Of course I can. I started carrying it a year ago. Asked Angeline's husband Sam to show me how to use it." She turned the blade, making it wink in the sunlight streaming in from the crack in the tarp. "He was a soldier in the war, like you."

Shane was glad to know she had asked someone she trusted. "You know it could get bloody."

"You do remember the sorry shape you were in when we first met?"

He grimaced. "Yes."

"Blood doesn't bother me. Neither does protecting what's mine."

Shane's heart skipped a beat. "And I'm yours to protect."

"Damn right." Her expression tightened. "I never had nothing that was mine. I aim to keep a hold of you for as long as I can."

Shane looked at Lettie and remembered all the things he used to have, the precious possessions he'd simply let go. He had been lucky, with a family, a home, and he'd pissed it away on whiskey. Shame washed over him. Lettie had endured a lifetime of nothing and was better than he was, a man who had everything and now had nothing.

She lived and worked with people who loved her, took care of her and kept her from harm. The world had been unkind to her for most of her life, and now she had the important things that mattered. He had thrown away all those gifts, and only now, sober for the first time in years, he saw all that he'd given up in this woman's eyes.

It wasn't the right time or place to have a life-changing moment, but it happened anyway. Shane shook from the power of the revelation. He had *everything,* and he gave it all up for *nothing.* Lettie had *nothing* and earned the right to *everything.* She was a stronger person than he ever was or would ever be. For the rest of his life, he would never forget this moment.

It was the moment Shane Murphy truly became a man.

This was what his pa and his sergeant had tried to teach him. Life was not happening *for* him, life was happening *to* him. Only he could steer the course, and if he chose to let the reins flap in the breeze, then he deserved all the bad that came with it. And oh how the bad had come and left him stripped bare, shivering in misery and stupidity.

Here he was in the back of a shitty wagon, covered in bruises, blood and sweat, with a woman he had fallen in love with. The Shane he was would have thrown up his hands and given Buster and his gang whatever they wanted. The Shane he was now would fight for his life and protect his lady or die trying.

His chest swelled with emotion, and he had to swallow a few dozen times before he embarrassed himself by saying something stupid. Lettie might have understood what he was feeling, but he wasn't ready to share it. If they made it out alive, he would tell her about it.

"Do you see that?" Buster shouted. "Some ijit left his horse by the side of the road. Probably taking a piss. Myron, go get it."

"I ain't stealing nobody's horse. That's a hanging crime, Buster." Myron knew how to whine.

"Don't be a pussy. Go get it and take Norman with you."

After another minute of whining, they heard the horses ride off to the right. Shane's gaze collided with Lettie's. Now was their chance to escape. She opened the side of the tarp and peered out.

Gone, she mouthed.

Shane looked out the side and nodded. There was no one there. They had to move fast since they had only a few minutes of time. He crept out far enough to see the ground. The wagon moved at a steady pace, but not slow. The ground had rocks aplenty, which was unfortunate considering they were barefoot. A group of trees stood to the right, and they had to get out of the wagon and make it to the tree line before the idiots realized what had happened.

He pulled back in and moved closer to Lettie. "Can you run?"

"I can do what I have to do. My legs ain't perfect, but if I'm being shot at, I can run."

The woman had grit. He was proud of her. "We've got to move fast. It's going to hurt when you land, so I think we should go feet first. As soon as you can get up, run for the trees to the right. Don't stop for anything."

"I'll do what you say, but don't think you can order me around every day. I don't take orders well."

"That's an understatement."

Lettie frowned at him, and he kissed her hard. "Let's go."

They both turned until they faced the front of the wagon and flipped onto their bellies. Then, like a pair of snakes, they shimmied backwards until their legs were hanging out the back of the wagon. The trick was in not letting Buster see what they were doing. If they did it right, the men wouldn't realize they were gone until arriving in Benson.

"Now." Shane launched himself out of the wagon. He landed on his feet then his knees with a painful thud. Lettie was already scrambling to stand. By the time he was upright, she was running for the trees as fast as the wind.

Shane was right behind her, fully expecting to feel the burn of a bullet in the back, but nothing happened. No shouts, no gunfire, no bullets. Shane and Lettie kept running deeper into the trees, faster and faster, until everything was a green blur. Branches whipped at them, roots reached up and tried to trip them, but still they ran.

Shane kept going until a stitch in his side hurt so bad, he could hardly get a breath in. He stopped and leaned against a tree, feebly wheezing her name. Lettie slowed to a stop, her bare feet crunching pine needles and oak leaves. She was breathing hard, her hair was in a frizzy halo, and strands stuck to the sweat on her face and neck. She limped as she walked toward him, and he wondered how her legs felt.

He was sure he looked a hell of a lot worse than she did, but it didn't matter. They had gotten away from the three morons, and if they were lucky, they would find their way to a town. He held up his hand and leaned against the tree, trying to catch his breath before he fell over in a heap.

She paced in a circle around the trees, her gaze straying to him over and over. Her breathing was normal long before his, and yet she said nothing. She obviously chose to love a man who couldn't run a couple miles without almost killing himself. The whiskey had nearly destroyed him inside and out. Plus he had been beaten twice in the last month. Lots of excuses, but none were important. He could only get better than who he was from now on.

The stitch finally receded from his side, and he was able to take in a deep breath. "We should get moving again. Buster followed us from Forestville for the money. He's not going to give it or us up that easily."

She ran her hands across her hair to try to tame it. He was startled to notice the condition of her fingers. They were red and bloodied, covered with scabs. His heart ached for what she'd put herself through to untie him, and all without saying a word of how much agony it caused her.

"Your fingers."

She glanced at them. "I've had worse."

"Not because of me."

"Oh don't think this was all because of you. I wanted to get out of there as bad as you." She put her hands behind her back. "Besides, I ain't got dainty feminine hands. I've had worse wounds than that. They'll heal."

"It doesn't matter if they'll heal. You did that for me." He tugged at her arms until he could see her hands again. One by one, he gently kissed each fingertip. She was the roughest diamond he'd ever encountered, but she was by far the most brilliant, dazzling, valuable treasure in the world.

"I didn't have anything better to do."

With a chuckle, he hugged her tight. When he let her go, he kissed her forehead, tasting the salt of her exertion. "How are your legs?"

"They hurt something powerful when I first started running. I think they're numb now. Standing still is making it worse." Her expression was one of controlled discomfort. He wished they could find a nice comfortable bed for a week and not come out until all their wounds, physical and emotional, were healed.

"We should get going."

"I ain't the one who had to stop." She gently touched the back of her thighs and hissed out a breath. "I need to get moving."

"What direction is Benson?"

"West. By my guess we were less than an hour from there by wagon."

"If we're lucky, that gives us less than an hour before Buster realizes we got away." Shane peered around them, noting they were heading north. "Do you know if there's a town close by?"

She shook her head. "I ain't left Forestville more than twice in a year, and both times we went to Benson."

"If we go east and head back home, he'll find us easy. Let's take a chance and keep heading in this direction then." He knew it was a risk to go on blindly, but they couldn't go south, or they would go back to the road, perhaps find the men waiting for them. This seemed to be the best choice, the only choice.

"What if we don't find a town?" She didn't sound scared, simply matter-of-fact.

"Then we keep going." He didn't want to walk for days; she probably couldn't. However they would do what they had to survive. It wasn't a choice but a matter of necessity.

"We'll need to find food and fresh water." She cocked her head and listened. "I don't hear any, but we may run across some."

"Sounds like you've done this before."

She didn't smile. "I've run and been chased like a rabbit. I know how to survive."

He had been a soldier, knew what it meant to survive and not only exist. Shane hadn't been chased like a rabbit, but he had been scared enough to feel like one. Considering the dire circumstances that generally accompanied them, a person never forgot survival skills.

"Then let's go."

They started running again, this time at a moderate pace that he could keep and that wouldn't cause her too much pain. Shane had no idea what they'd find, but they were on their way. The woods were cool, letting only dappled sunlight through. The only noises were their footsteps crackling through the heavy layer of pine needles, sticks and leaves. Occasionally a bird tweeted or a squirrel chattered.

Another half an hour passed in silence before Lettie came

to a stop. She was breathing hard and sweat ran down her face, staining her brown dress under the arms and breasts. She'd never looked better to him.

"I hear water."

"Thank God, because I'm parched." He sucked in air, disturbed that he didn't hear the water. She must have hearing like a bat.

"To the left." She walked slowly and deliberately. He realized she was keeping her approach as quiet as possible.

"What are you doing?"

"Shush."

She went around the side of a big clump of bushes and disappeared. Shane walked where she had, respecting the fact she wanted to be silent. He found her standing beside a small creek, watching the water flow past.

He stopped beside her. "What are you doing?"

"I reckon you haven't spent much time in the woods."

"Mostly lived on the plains, on a farm. In the war, I did what they told me to. I didn't have to do the finding or nothing." Soldiering was hard, and he had hated it. He could build a fire, chop wood, plant a field, milk a cow but hadn't had to search for fresh water in the forest. There weren't many forests like this in the plains where he grew up.

"When you find water, you need to be sure it's safe. If there are critters about or have been here, it's drinkable. If too many of them are using it to shit in and around, you don't want to be drinking it." She pointed to tracks in the mud. "Those are raccoon tracks, and over there is likely a bobcat."

"Good or bad?" He had no idea there was so much that went in to figuring out if he could drink water or not. His mouth watered at the sight of the creek, and he sure as hell didn't want to wait much longer.

"Good." She got to her knees gently with a grimace, then she scooped up a handful of water and slurped it. "It tastes good too."

Shane didn't wait a second longer. He almost stuck his head in the creek, drinking great gulps of water. His stomach cramped, protesting the gorging. He lay back on the carpet of leaves, trying like hell not to bring the water back up.

She hovered over him. "If you puke on me again, I might have to punch you, Murphy."

He laughed, albeit with a bit of pain. "I'm sorry. I was so damn thirsty. I forgot how sick I was gonna get."

"I drank my fill and you obviously did. We need to go." Her mouth drew down into a frown. "I don't want to be anyplace they might be looking for us."

Shane had forgotten for one blessed minute that they were running because of the threat from Buster and his men. Sitting there and smiling at her, alone, was reminiscent of their time in the stream earlier that day. He ached to be back there, making love to her in the cool flow of water.

He got to his feet and blew out a breath. "Your legs?"

She shrugged. "Bearable."

That one word was full of meaning, so much so he couldn't sort through it. Now that he knew what she'd endured in her life, bearable was more than likely completely unbearable for most people.

"If it gets to be too much, tell me. The sun is starting to go down. It will be pure dark soon. We need to find shelter." His stomach grumbled, and he wished they still had the basket of food from the restaurant. He might be able to get a rabbit after they found a place to spend the night. "I can carry you."

She made a scoffing sound, and without a word she started walking with a significant limp. The woman had been running on wounded legs for an hour or more. Now she was refusing his help, when she could hardly stay upright. Stubborn wench.

Well he could not talk too. Shane needed to be a man, and that meant doing what needed to be done. He caught up to her, and before she could protest, scooped her into his arms and starting running. When it was only his weight, he struggled, but with her depending on him, he felt like he could run to Utah and back.

"Put me down."

"We had this conversation, Lettie. I ain't putting you down, so shut up and let me do what I gotta do."

She made all kinds of noises, grumbles, curses, snorts and dramatic sighs, but she didn't struggle against his hold. He was glad of it, since he didn't have the breath to argue with her. For once, Shane felt in control around her. A fleeting experience, but it felt damn good.

Sweat trickled down every surface of his body, even his nose, but he kept going. They would have to stop soon or he might just kill both of them when he collapsed.

"There, beneath the leaves." She squinted ahead and pointed. "I see something shiny, like a window."

He slowed down and headed in the direction she pointed. By the time they got close, he recognized the outline of a shack. The forest had begun to swallow the building. The leaves and trees hung over the roof, covering it almost completely.

Shane set Lettie down in a soft patch of grass and went to explore the cabin. "I need your knife."

With a grimace, she pulled it from the scabbard and handed it to him. He could almost feel her complaints at being left behind, but she probably couldn't walk if she wanted to.

The door was open an inch, but vines had grown in and around the frame. Surprisingly the window was intact, if not filthier than him. He used her knife to cut away the leaves and branches and clear the door, then the window, as best he could. It took a good five minutes of yanking before it opened enough for him to get through.

The inside smelled dusty and deserted, but dry. Someone had spent time putting down a wood floor, which now heaved up in various places. The cabin was no more than fifteen foot wide in any direction, but it had been well made a very long time ago. Weak sunlight filtered through the dirty window. There was a broken chair but otherwise no furniture. The chair could be firewood, and the dust could be swept aside with a branch of leaves. It was perfect.

Lettie gritted her teeth. Her legs throbbed in a steady beat with her pulse, which rushed past her ears. *Thump, thump, thump.* There wasn't a part of her that didn't hurt in some way. Aches, pains and bruises she could usually ignore. The stabbing agony in her legs was not so easy to ignore.

She wouldn't tell Shane, but she'd been grateful when he picked her up and carried her, to the point where she almost wept happy tears. That surely would have been something. Walking or running any farther was impossible. She would have done it because she had to. She was grateful she didn't. The shack they found was a lucky coincidence. It was well hidden in the trees. Someone like Buster wasn't smart enough to notice it there. She hoped.

After a few minutes of sitting, she was glad not to be bouncing in Shane's arms. That didn't mean she hurt any less, but she wasn't hurting any more. The forest was full of nature, crickets were singing, frogs croaking and there were a few birds still chirping.

A small bird hopped toward her, its head cocked. Closer and closer it moved until she could see it was a sparrow. She stared at the bird, hoping like hell it was a coincidence. A sparrow? It had to mean nothing or would mean everything. The feather from her pillow sat nestled in the chest of drawers at home.

Lettie closed her eyes, unable to think straight. Later she would try to puzzle out the sparrow and the damn feather. For now, she leaned against the trunk of the tree and shut her eyes to rest.

When Shane appeared in front of her, she was startled. He smiled and picked her up again. She had gotten used to him being shirtless, but touching his bare skin still brought a tiny thrill. "I didn't want to wake you, but the shack is dry and a good place to rest and stay the night."

She glanced around, surprised to see time had passed since she'd thought about the peacefulness of the forest. "I fell asleep?"

"Yep, I believe you did. It gave me time to clean up a little and put together a bed for us." He turned sideways and carried her into the shack. The light was murky, but it was enough to see what was there.

Lettie couldn't explain it, but she felt safe inside it. The perfectly square building held nothing but a bed made of large green leaves in the middle of it and a broken chair. Yet it welcomed her and gave her a sense of belonging. How that was possible, she didn't know. There were a lot of things that had happened in the last month she couldn't explain, and likely never would.

He set her on the bed of cool green leaves. He'd made it a few inches thick, and it was quite comfortable. Shane reached behind him and came up with a leaf full of berries of different sizes. Her stomach rumbled loud and long. He laughed and put the leaf in her lap.

"Eat."

There he was ordering her around again. At the moment, she was too hungry to tell him not to do it again, so she dug into the berries. The flavor burst in her mouth, and she greedily ate every one of them. Shane watched her with a grin playing around his lips.

She narrowed her eyes. "Did you give me all the food?"

"No, I ate as I picked. Didn't find one rabbit out there, which was okay because I couldn't find anything to start a fire." He shrugged. "I went searching for what we could eat. There are berry bushes all around the cabin, heavy with fruit. I can get more if you're still hungry." There was the grin again.

"Then why are you smiling?"

His grin grew wider. "You have berry juice all over your face."

Her first instinct was to scrub it off with her sleeve. Instead, she thrust up her chin and challenged him. "Then clean me up."

His brows went up. "Is that an order?"

"I thought I'd return yours in kind."

He got to his feet and bowed. "As you wish, my lady."

My lady.

Was she his lady? She sure as hell wanted to be his lady. Neither one of them would find a mate as perfect if they searched for a hundred years. He was her man, and that fact would never change no matter what happened.

"I found a short waterfall behind the cabin, with a small pool beneath it. Only about a foot deep and three feet wide, but the water seemed clean. I need to find something to carry water in." He knelt beside her, cupped her face and kissed her senseless. His tongue traced the outline of her mouth, then delved inside to dance with hers. Sweet, hot, wet kisses she could drown in.

When he pulled away, her heart was beating hard for a very different reason, and damned if her nipples weren't aching to be touched and her pussy wet in anticipation.

"You taste good, Lettie." He kissed all around her mouth, punctuated with little licks.

"You kiss good, Shane." Her voice was breathy. She wanted more. She wanted to feel him inside her again, filling her, bringing her the most exquisite pleasure she'd never known existed.

How crazy to want to be with him. She could barely walk, was covered in sweat and dirt, yet she needed him. He seemed to understand, and his expression softened.

"Let me get some water and I can wash you up."

"Hate to tell you, Murphy, but you need to wash too."

He glanced down at his bare, dirty chest. "I probably stink too."

"I wasn't going to say anything."

He grinned and kissed her again, hard and fast. "I'll be right back."

Lettie lay back on the leaves, surprised by how comfortable they were. Her eyes fluttered closed, and she let herself drift. Although they were being chased, were running for their lives, she felt safe with Shane. Safe enough to fall asleep.

The next time she woke, shadows had overtaken the cabin. Lettie panicked for a moment before she felt a warm body beside hers and recognized his scent.

Shane.

The entire day came flooding back at her, filled with emotion, danger, love, pleasure, fear and acceptance. It was a day she could never forget. Her life had changed in the last twenty-four hours, of that she was certain. What the future held was uncertain. She knew she wanted to be with Shane, and he seemed to want to be with her.

They were lost, in the middle of a forest in Wyoming, without food, water, shoes or a shirt for him to wear. Her wounds were waking up too. They needed doctoring besides Shane's field dressing. She should be tied in knots with worry, but lying there beside him in the tiny cabin, she felt calm. It was pure magic the way they fit together like two pieces of a puzzle. Comfortable, safe, perfect.

She must have made a noise or perhaps he sensed she was awake because he spoke into the gloom.

"Lettie?"

"I'm here." She couldn't imagine being anyplace else.

"Are you feeling okay? Do you need anything?"

She chuckled into the darkness. "You sound like Marta."

"I hope you don't get us confused."

Lettie laughed this time. "I reckon that won't happen."

"Good, because I don't want you kissing her accidentally." Shane's breath was warm against her cheek.

"That ain't a possibility." She turned her head until she thought she was face-to-face with him. "I only want to kiss you."

His lips found hers, a little to the left, but he corrected it and kissed her softly. "And I only want to kiss you."

"I want to do more than kiss. My tits are aching, and my pussy is too."

He was silent for a moment. "You are honest, that's for sure."

She reached over and found his cock, pulsing and hard in his trousers. "Seems like you are needing more than kissing too."

He sucked in a breath, and she started to move her hand up and down his staff. She loved the feel of his hardness beneath her fingers. It was life. It was love. It was pleasure.

"Every time I'm around you, my dick gets hard. Hell, that first day in the bath, the first time you touched me, I couldn't control it." His voice was thick with what she thought was passion.

"Then don't."

He rolled onto his side, creating an awkward angle for her to keep touching him. "I don't want to hurt you."

"The only way you'll hurt me is if you don't touch me. Please, Shane." She swallowed her pride, using *please* again with him. "I need you to touch me."

"I can pleasure you, honey. Let me make you feel good." He nibbled on her earlobe, something she was coming to realize was her weakness.

Shivers rolled down her body, and a throb in her lower belly turned into an ache in her nether regions. "Yes. Make me feel good."

He shifted beside her, and she still couldn't see a thing. "What are you doing?"

"Shush, woman." A few more moments passed, and he unbuttoned her dress. Her nipples grew impossibly taut, and she could barely contain her impatience.

He took his time undressing her, one piece at a time, kissing her exposed skin when she least expected it. It raised her arousal with each unexpected touch of his lips. She moaned when he kissed her belly. She squirmed when he kissed her hip. Slowly, and with great care, he undressed her completely.

Naked in the black night, Lettie would have been afraid a month ago. Now she could hardly wait to see what he would do next. When the wet, cool cloth touched her shoulder, she sighed with pleasure.

He was washing her.

It might have been strange to anyone else, but she loved it. She was covered with sweat and dirt, and the feel of the cloth against her skin was pleasurable. The fact he was the person cleaning her, whereas she had cleaned him weeks ago, made their relationship a full circle. They had started this way and here they were again, going in the opposite direction.

He cleaned each breast, avoiding her nipples, much to her consternation. His tongue swiped one and the other, and she about melted. His hot tongue bathed her nipples over and over, then his teeth nibbled at her. Lettie arched up into his mouth, eager for more.

He continued washing her, moving down her stomach, closer and closer to her aching pussy. He avoided it, as he had her nipples, and cleaned her legs and feet. After untying the bandages around her thighs, he gently washed the wounds. He tied what she hoped was clean bandages around them. He must have cut her petticoat up as she'd asked. The man made her heart flutter with each act of love he performed. How could she have ever thought he was a drunken fool?

"I didn't hurt you, did I?"

She *tsk*ed at him. "You'll only hurt me if you don't start cleaning my woman parts right quick."

He made a strangled sound again. "As you wish, my lady," he repeated.

178

His hands grazed her thighs, raising goose bumps as his calloused fingers skimmed along her tender skin. He spread her legs, allowing the cool air to caress her heated core. He breathed in through his nose loud enough for her to hear it, then he kissed her there. Between her legs.

She couldn't stop the gasp that popped out of her mouth. "Do people really do that? I thought it was only in dreams."

"Shush, woman." He placed the cool cloth against her, gently cleaning the most private part of her body. It felt wonderful but not as good as his lips on her.

Lettie hoped he would do it again. And again. And again.

After thoroughly cleaning her and raising her arousal level to near frantic, he touched her thighs with his hands. She almost sighed when his hot breath caressed her aching flesh.

He spread her nether lips and blew. She clenched so tight, it sent a bolt of pleasure through her.

"I wish I could see you."

"It ain't pretty. It's a regular pussy, Shane." She didn't know what she was saying, so eager to have him touch her more.

He chuckled. "It's more than regular. It's yours."

With that, he licked her slit from top to bottom. Lettie stopped breathing for a moment as the sheer ecstasy of his touch rippled through her.

"Jesus Christ."

"Nope. Shane." This time his tongue slid inside her like a little cock.

Lettie dug her fingers into the leaves beneath her, their soft wetness crumpling in her grip. He found the nubbin of pleasure hidden in the folds of her pussy and sucked at it.

She nearly cried for him never to stop. It felt incredible, the most incredible thing she'd ever imagined. His thumbs slid inside her, fucking her with a steady rhythm that matched the draw of his mouth.

His tongue tickled her clit as he sucked. With each beat, her hands clenched harder, her heart thumped against her ribs and her tits ached to be touched. She reached for her nipples, desperate for more. The first time she pinched herself, she gasped.

He paused and pulled his mouth away. "Are you touching yourself?"

Not even a little embarrassed, she answered, "Yes, dammit, because you can't pleasure my cunt at the same time as my tits. I need both."

He was silent for a moment, her hot pussy pulsing not an inch from his talented mouth. "God, I love you, woman."

His words combined with her arousal made her eyes sting with unshed tears. "Then show me."

He didn't need instructions, that was for sure. His mouth descended on her, his tongue working, licking, sucking, teasing her.

Lick. Suck. Lick. Suck. Nibble.

His teeth closed around her nubbin, and she pinched her nipples hard enough to cause a smidgen of pain. It actually raised her pleasure higher, so she did it at the same time as he bit her.

When her orgasm hit, it was with the force of a twister. She bucked against him, squeezing his head with her thighs. A silent scream ripped through her along with exquisite ecstasy. The waves of pleasure went on and on, as he continued to lick, suck and nibble at her, his thumbs fucking her.

When she finally gained her breath back, she whimpered,

but he kept his mouth on her. She couldn't take a second more.

"Please, Shane, stop."

He didn't answer, but he kept sucking and licking at her. To her astonishment, another orgasm built quickly. It was less intense than the first, but longer, as though she were under a waterfall and the water drenched her over and over. She cried out his name, her voice choked with love.

Shane gentled his mouth until he was only kissing her softly, bringing her back down from the stars. He kissed her one last time, snaking his tongue out to tickle her clit. She jerked from the sensation, and he chuckled. She would have yelled at him if she had a voice. Instead she floated lethargically on the ripples moving through her as though the two powerful orgasms hadn't left her body.

He closed her thighs, then kissed his way up her belly to her breasts. When his mouth closed around one breast, she groaned. With a few sucks and licks, he shifted to the other to repeat the process.

"I couldn't help myself. I needed to taste them too." He settled beside her and leaned over to kiss her. His breath and lips tasted musky, and she realized it was her. This was so different than what she'd experienced so long ago, another lifetime, with Angeline and the forced sex. Shane had pleasured her, and she found herself curious and feeling naughtier by the second. She pulled his head down to hers and kissed him. She lapped at his lips until he opened them.

A rich tanginess filled his mouth, and she pulled it into her own, excited by the fact he had shared her essence and it tasted as forbidden as it was thrilling. She kissed him thoroughly, her body pushing against his, skin to skin. But not all of him was bare. He still wore his trousers, his cock hard and pulsing against her hip.

"Make love to me."

"You're not ready for that, Lettie. You're still covered in bruises and wounds." His voice sounded strained. "I can't."

She reached for him, but he moved backwards. "You will let me touch you."

"No, I don't, ah, Jesus…"

Her hand curled around his member, rendering him mute. While he made noises in his throat, she unbuttoned his trousers and freed him from the confines of the fabric. He was so warm and hard, filling her hands with man. She tightened her grip but didn't know what to do next.

"Rub it up and down, yeah, that's it, faster, harder," he commanded with breathless intensity.

She heightened his arousal with each squeeze and tug, with each breath against her cheek. Lettie was in control, pulling him toward his release. His scent surrounded her, filled her with heat and love.

He stiffened beside her, his fingers digging into her hip. "Ah, God, Lettie, I'm coming."

His cock erupted in her hand, the warm streams of life running down her fingers. Knowing she was the reason he had found his ultimate pleasure, that she was the person to bring him there, filled her with joy.

This was what she was missing, the piece she never understood that existed between Sam and Angeline. She'd witnessed it but never quite knew what it all meant. Until now. Until she found pleasure with the man she loved in the shadows of a cabin being swallowed by the forest.

Lettie finally knew what joy was.

"I can't believe I let you do that."

She smiled at him. "I don't think you could've stopped me."

He barked a laugh. "No, I don't think so either. Stay right there."

She lay there, naked and satiated, while he cleaned her hands and redressed her in her chemise, using her dress as a blanket. She listened to him perform his ablutions, the chink of his suspenders, and the splash of the water. All the while, she floated on air.

Shane settled in beside her, his big body warming hers to a comfortable level. As Lettie drifted off to sleep, she wondered if she could hold on to the joy for the rest of her life.

Angeline woke up to the sound of knocking. Loud, insistent knocking. Sam roused beside her and lit a candle. She blinked at him sleepily.

"Is someone knocking?"

Bang, bang, bang.

"Yep, sounds like it." Sam yawned and started to get out of bed.

Angeline blew the sleep from her mind and came fully awake. No one knocked on their door in the middle of the night. Something was wrong.

She jumped out of bed and threw on the dress from the chair, ignoring Sam's startled shout. Angeline nearly flew down the stairs to the front door, yanking it open breathlessly. Pieter stood there, his bushy eyebrows in a serious scowl.

"Lettie and Shane did not come back to the Blue Plate. Marta wired to the store in Benson, and they did not arrive."

Dread coiled its way around her stomach, and she curled her hands around her belly, a protective instinct for her child. "What happened?"

"I don't know, but they are missing. I talk to Hans at livery. He said wagon needed a new wheel, but he didn't have money to replace." Pieter's accent grew heavier the faster he talked. "Marta thinks they had an accident."

"Sweet Jesus." Angeline pressed her hand to her mouth, afraid for her friend and the man who had captured her heart. She had pushed Lettie into going when she hadn't really wanted to.

Sam stood behind her and put his hands on her shoulders. "When are we leaving?"

"An hour. Be at the restaurant." Pieter disappeared into the darkness, the lantern in his hand the only light in the inky night.

"I'm going with you."

"Oh no you're not." Sam closed the door, making the candle flicker in the breeze. It illuminated his expression, casting shadows on his beloved yet worried face.

"Yes I am. If they had an accident, they'll need someone to doctor them. I'm going, and there isn't a thing you can do to stop me." Angeline marched past him, her nose in the air, daring him to contradict her. She would make coffee and get ready to leave.

Lettie was her sister as much as Eliza was. Angeline would leave with the men who went in search of the couple. They would have to tie her down to keep her home.

Lettie needed her, and she would go no matter what.

Chapter Eight

A flock of birds screeched outside, waking Shane from his slumber. Daylight filtered in weakly through the tiny cabin window. He hadn't slept so deeply in his entire life. It had to be due to the woman who lay beside him, the woman who owned his heart.

Her face was relaxed in sleep, making her look much younger than she was. The frown lines were gone, and her thick lashes lay like miniature fans on her cheeks. Her mouth was slightly open and those lips, those luscious lips, called to him. He leaned over to kiss her when he heard a voice.

He scrambled to his feet, his instincts on alert. He ran for the window, keeping to the shadows. The glass was still dirty enough to make it hard to see out, but he cleaned a corner, enough to peer outside. He was glad he'd used a sturdy branch to bar the door last night. The door was hard enough to open, but with the stick there, it would be impossible.

Shane pressed his cheek to the corner of the window and looked out. At first he saw nothing amiss, the green of the woods and the trees standing in the early morning sun. His heart thundered and his mouth went cotton dry. Sweat trickled down his back as he watched and waited. He spotted movement beyond the clearing.

Shit. If Buster and his men were out there, Shane and Lettie were trapped. There was only one way in and one way out of the small cabin. If they were lucky, none of the men would spot the tiny building hidden in the folds of the leaves and trees. Of course, lucky had never been a word used to describe either Shane or Lettie.

He crept back across the cabin, keeping low. When he reached Lettie, he placed his hand across her mouth. "Someone's outside."

Before she could react or protest, he scooped her up and carried her to the darkest corner, to the right of the door where no one could possibly see her even if they looked through the filthy window. Protecting Lettie had become his mission, and he'd be damned if he'd fail now.

He retrieved her brown dress, vowing to burn it one day, and handed it to her. Scuttling around the cabin like a bug, he scattered the leaves to give the appearance of randomness. He wanted no evidence that anyone had been there. Sweating and shaking, Shane returned to Lettie and sat holding her knife in his hand.

The minutes ticked by, and all he heard were vague noises in the woods beyond. The unfortunate fact was the very leaves and trees that were swallowing the cabin also insulated it against noise. No one could hear them, but they couldn't hear much either. It didn't help the tension one bit.

Lettie leaned over and whispered, "Is it Buster?"

He cupped his hand around her ear and spoke softly. "I don't know. We're safe unless they realize we're in here, then all they have to do is break the glass."

They sat there, as still as possible, for what seemed like an exceptionally long time. Shane's legs started to cramp, and he was sure she was even more uncomfortable. Yet they waited in the shadows, angry and scared.

When someone knocked on the door, both of them flinched but managed not to make a sound to give themselves away. Shane didn't know if he was shaking or if it was Lettie, but someone sure as hell was shaking.

"Is anyone in there?" It was a woman's voice, or at least it could have been a woman. Definitely wasn't one of the three men. "I seen blood out here on the leaves and thought mebbe somebody was hurt."

Shane met Lettie's gaze in the gray gloom. They could trust that the stranger was alone and could help. Or they could stay put until she went away, leaving them still stranded and lost. When Lettie nodded at him, he knew she'd come to the same conclusion. They had to take a chance or the next people to find them really could be the three troublemakers who hunted them.

He got to his feet and walked to the door. "Who's out there?"

"Oh you are in there. This old cabin doesn't let many folks in y'know." A cackling laugh. "You must be somepin' special."

"Who are you?"

"I'm Mountain Marge, down to get supplies in Benson. I saw blood and thought I could help. I learned medicines from the Injuns when I was a girl." She paused. "If'n you don't want help, I'll be on my way."

Shane pulled the branch from the door and managed to open it. When he stepped into the light, he saw a woman no bigger than a child, wearing a pair of trousers rolled up and secured with a rope. Her dirt-brown shirt was also rolled up and tied together to stay on her frame. She wore a floppy, ugly hat and carried a potato sack on one shoulder. Her wrinkled face lit up in a smile when she spotted him.

"Well, I never expected to find a young, handsome buck shirtless at the door." She cackled again. "You are somepin' special."

He scanned the woods behind her, but he saw nothing beyond a sparrow on a branch. "Are you alone?"

She glanced behind. "You don't see nobody, do you? A'course I'm alone. Mountain Marge doesn't travel with anyone." She peered at his bare chest. "You need doctoring?"

"No but my wife does. We had a wagon accident yesterday, and it landed on her legs."

"Broke?" Mountain Marge pushed past him into the cabin. "Let me take a gander at her."

Just like that, they had help. Shane was so relieved Marge had found them he hopped to her every command while she examined Lettie's wounds. She pronounced Shane's field dressing "pretty dang good". She didn't have a horse, but she had a mule "over yonder" and offered to guide them to Benson.

Shane looked at Lettie, and she frowned. "We, uh, were headed to Benson, but three men tried to rob us. Home is Forestville. We need to get there instead."

"I wondered about the rope marks on your wrists and feet." Marge nodded sagely. "There's some bad folks round these parts. I wouldn't go to Benson either. We's within a half a day's ride from Forestville. I can take you there if you like."

Shane could have wept from the news they were so close to home. "Yes, ma'am, that'd be right fine."

"The store there ain't as good as the one in Benson, so I don't generally go there. I'll help you folks get home though. Your woman can ride old Bertha. She's a good mule." Marge eyed Shane again, her gaze traveling up and down his torso. "And I can get my fill of looking at you along the way."

Lettie laughed, hooting like she'd never heard something so funny. Shane wanted a shirt.

"Let's get a move on then." Marge got to her feet. "I reckon we don't want those three bad'uns to find us."

Shane picked up Lettie and followed the tiny mountain

woman out the door. Lettie wound her arms around his neck and leaned into him.

"I love you, Shane Murphy." Her soft whisper echoed through him as though she'd shouted.

He kissed her ear and whispered, "I love you too, Lettie Brown."

Bertha the mule seemed to be older than Mountain Marge, impossible as it was. Yet she allowed Shane to set Lettie on her sideways. There were empty sacks hanging from the ropes that held the blanket on the mule's back. He assumed Marge would fill those with supplies and bring them to her mountain home. Shane would make sure they were full to bursting for what she'd done for them.

The ride through the woods was less frantic than the day before, and with considerably less panic. Shane walked along, his feet sore but not too bad. The fresh air filled his lungs, and he had a tiny flame of hope inside him that the nightmare was over. The birds sang, the sun graced the forest with warmth and things were going well. When they reached the road that would lead them back to Forestville, everything went wrong at once.

He should have expected it, but he hadn't.

Buster, Myron and Norman were in the middle of the road blocking their passage home. Their pistols were pointed at the three ragtag travelers. Another flock of birds burst from the woods, cawing as their black wings winked in the bright sunlight.

Shane had no chance against three armed men considering he had nothing but a knife. Dammit to hell. Greed drove men to be ruthless bastards.

"Shit," Mountain Marge offered. "I'm guessing that's the three you been hiding from."

"You'd be right." Shane didn't take his gaze off the three troublemakers. He gripped the knife, knowing he couldn't do much damage before the bullets ripped into the women who were now in his care.

"You're a clever two, ain't ya?" Buster sneered. "I don't know how you got out of that wagon, but I aim to get the money. Now."

"We don't have it, fool." Lettie sneered right back. "It's at the bank in Benson. Bet you had some trouble when you got there and couldn't get it, hmm?"

"Shut up, bitch." Buster cocked his pistol and pointed it straight at Lettie.

Shane accepted he had only moments to live, but he could die knowing he had fallen in love with a good woman, had a taste of what true joy was. He would die for her, without question or hesitation.

He stepped in front of the mule, blocking Buster from getting off a good shot. "Go back to the hole you climbed out of. We won't send the law after you, and you can go back to ranching."

Buster laughed without humor. "You think it's that easy? Hell no. You done humiliated me and my boys here. We ain't gonna let you go this time. We're going to kill the both of you and enjoy the deed."

Lettie kept egging him on. "What about the money? Don't you want it? If you kill us, you won't ever get it."

"Oh I'll make sure I hurt you good and make you tell me the truth. I aim to get that money, fuck you until you bleed, then kill you. Bitch." Buster now aimed for Shane. "But first I'm gonna enjoy killing your man here."

The first shot ripped through Shane's shoulder. He threw the knife before he turned to slap the mule's rump and send it running in the other direction. Mountain Marge screeched and ran toward the men, a shotgun appearing from her skirt. Buster's second shot tore into Shane's gut.

All hell broke loose, and he saw others ride in from behind the three bandits. One of the riders was Angeline, her blonde hair gleaming in the sun. He fell to his knees, lightheaded and woozy. When he saw the knife protruding from Norman's leg, Shane smiled.

Then his face said howdy to the road and everything went black.

Lettie stood at the window, staring out into the evening sky. Vibrant pinks, oranges and reds painted the sides of the buildings in Forestville. She should have appreciated the beauty of the sunset, but her heart was occupied with the man who lay inert on the bed.

It was the same bed he had been in the first time they spoke, in the room where they first started to fall in love. This time his injury was because of her. It wasn't a nameless, faceless bastard who beat him. No, it was Buster Dawson, the man she'd jeered at, discounted as a fool, who had shot Shane down like a dog.

Her throat closed up, and she blinked back tears. She'd done enough crying for his injury, screaming and carrying on like a madwoman until Sam had pulled her off the bleeding Shane. Her overreaction nearly cost him his life.

Now she sat by his side, changing his bandages, wiping him down with cool cloths as his body fought the fever that had set in almost immediately. He'd had to ride a horse back to Forestville with a bullet in his shoulder and belly. Stomach wounds were the worst. The doctor had worked for hours repairing the damage done by the bullet.

Two days had passed, and Shane fought against infection and fever. Lettie had been there every second, willing him to live. If he didn't, her heart would never recover. Hers beat with each thump of his, steady and strong in his chest. He was unconscious, lost in a world where she couldn't reach him. Each second that ticked by was excruciating.

"Lettie?"

She didn't turn around when she heard Angeline's voice. "I wouldn't be anyplace else."

"You need to eat." Angeline stepped up beside her. "He wouldn't want you to make yourself sick."

"I'm not hungry." She hadn't had much appetite for days. All she did was take care of Shane and hope she hadn't given her love to a man only to have him snatched from her arms only days later. Her stomach churned with fear and rage.

She had no one to be angry at except Buster and his cohorts, and he had already been brought to Laramie to stand trial for attempted murder. Sam convinced the marshals to transport him and his men before Lettie got to them. He had done the right thing because she would have killed them if Shane died. She might even kill them for putting them both through this pain.

"I knew you'd say that so I brought the food with me." Angeline set a bowl of stew on the chest of drawers and pulled Lettie over to the chair beside the bed. "You can sit here and feed yourself while he heals."

Lettie didn't want to, but she was feeling a little sick from eating nothing. She let Angeline sit her down and give her the bowl. The salty scent filled her nose, and to Lettie's surprise, her stomach rumbled noisily. She took a spoonful and was grateful when she was able to swallow it.

Angeline smiled and sat on the edge of the bed. She looked at Shane lying motionless beneath the white sheets. "He looks better, like he has more color."

Lettie swallowed the second bite and gazed at Shane's whiskered face. His cheeks looked gaunt and sunken, his eyes too. He had been pink with fever, but it had broken an hour earlier. She took another bite of stew and realized Angeline was right. He did appear as though he had a more natural color to his face.

"His fever broke?"

"About an hour ago." Lettie set the bowl down after four bites. It was enough. "I cried." Her voice broke on the last word, and she had to swallow hard not to cry again.

Angeline stood and held out her hand. Lettie got to her feet and let her friend pull her into a hug, a nice hard one. Exactly what she needed, even if she wouldn't admit it. She hung on, fighting her exhaustion and her emotions. Who knew that hugs would become so important?

"He'll be okay, Lettie. The man survived the fever and the surgery. He's strong and young." Angeline's soft voice calmed Lettie as much as the hug.

"I can't lose him, Angeline. I can't." Lettie leaned back and stared into her friend's eyes. "I didn't think I could love a man. I never knew what it felt like or imagined how much he would mean to me."

"Does this mean you'll marry me?" Shane's gravelly voice made both women jump.

Much to her consternation, she cried again, falling to her knees beside the bed. She barely saw Angeline leave the room and close the door behind her.

His hand landed on her head, and he petted her hair. "You look like hell."

193

She laughed and wiped away her tears with angry swipes. "You sure can flatter a girl."

"I know what my girl likes to hear." His grin was crooked.

Lettie took a few deep breaths to tuck the emotions back into place, before she could speak again. It was difficult, but she managed to stop the tears although her throat was tight, holding back the dam that threatened to burst.

"You almost died. The doc spent two hours digging those bullets out and fixing your belly." She pointed to the wound on his shoulder. "That was the bleeder and the reason you almost died. There was so much blood."

"I thought blood didn't bother you." His eyes drooped, and his voice faded with each word.

"It don't, except if it's yours. Hell, you started out by bleeding and puking on me. I thought it was good you only bled on me this time." She had never felt so out of control than she did at that moment.

Lettie loved Shane, something she never expected. Yet almost losing him because he protected her was nearly too much to bear. If this was what love was, she didn't know if she wanted it. Better to live miserably than to die a little each day because someone she loved was hurt or in danger. She was being torn in two by her cowardice and her heart.

"I still want to marry you." His eyes drifted closed into sleep.

Marriage was a prospect Lettie did not welcome. After her disastrous first marriage, she expected it to be her last. Now he'd said twice that he wanted to marry her. Her stomach clenched at the thought. She pressed her face into his hand, breathing in his scent, his life. He had practically sacrificed himself for her. How could she let that happen again? Would she survive it?

Whirling with emotions she didn't want or welcome, Lettie left the room for the first time in two days. Now that he slept instead of laying unconscious, she could go home and take a bath then sleep. She needed to be away from him to clear her head and decide what to do about the man who owned her heart.

When she stepped outside the Blue Plate to walk home, she was surprised to find Mountain Marge waiting with her mule. She raised her hand in greeting.

"Hey there, Lettie. I was gettin' ready to head on home, but I wanted to say goodbye to ya and yer man." The old woman had various full packs on the back of her mule.

Marta and Pieter had offered her a room for a few days and compensated her with supplies for helping Shane and Lettie. The hermit had gotten along well with the German couple, and Lettie expected Mountain Marge would be back.

"He's doing better. He just woke up." A tremor sounded in her voice. "I, uh, am headed home to get some sleep."

Marge took her hands, peering up at Lettie from her tiny height. "That's a good'un, right there. You take care of him, y'hear? The good'uns don't come around often."

With that, the mountain inhabitant released Lettie's hands and turned to pick up the mule's reins.

"Thank you for everything, Marge. We wouldn't have survived without you." Lettie owed the woman a debt, and she wouldn't forget that.

Marge waved her hand in dismissal. "Pshaw. 'Tweren't nothing. You keep yourself safe, Lettie."

Lettie watched her amble away chatting with the mule and sidestepping piles of horse droppings in the road. Life was simple for Marge. If only it was for Lettie.

Emma Lang

Shane woke to bright sunshine and birds twittering. He opened his eyes slowly and recognized his room at the restaurant. There was a staleness to the air, as though the room had been closed up for days. He remembered Lettie beside the bed crying and an ache in his gut, but not much else.

He tried to move, and pain shot through him like a white-hot poker. Memories of the fight with Buster and his men flooded Shane's brain. He'd been shot twice by the lousy son of a bitch.

"Ah, you are awake, *liebchen*." Marta appeared beside the bed, smiling. Her apple cheeks were as rosy as always. The fact she called him *liebchen* did not escape his notice. "Lettie said you had woken last night and asked us to look over you. Poor child hasn't slept in days, sitting here taking care of you. She needed to go home and rest."

Days? Shane ran his hand down his face and was surprised to find a full crop of whiskers. He was in worse shape than he thought.

"Is she okay?" He thought perhaps Lettie had spent days by his side without sleeping. She didn't need to make herself sick by taking care of him.

"Ach, she is fine. Once your fever broke, she was wrung out. I sent her home to bed, and we took turns checking on you last night." Marta sat on the side of the bed. "I can check your wounds now, ya?"

Shane nodded, and the older woman got to work. She was very gentle, removing soiled bandages and wrapping fresh ones around his wounds. The shoulder wound ached, but the gut wound hurt like mad. It would be a long time before it healed, if it healed proper at all.

196

"What did the doc say?" He was worried, he'd admit it. During the war a gut wound could kill a man quick or fester for two weeks and then a fella could die in agony. Shane didn't want either to happen.

"He said you lost a lot of blood, but you were strong. Lettie took care of you good. She did everything the doctor say. It is her who saved you." Marta gathered up the bandages and got to her feet. "I will send Karen up with breakfast, if you are up to eating."

He was mildly hungry, more tired, but food did sound good right about then. "That sounds wonderful, Mrs. Gunderson. Thank you."

She smiled and headed for the door. "You are family now, *liebchen*. There is no thanks when you are family."

He stared at the door long after she went through it, shocked by Marta's pronouncement. He was family? How did he get to be family in less than a month? It must have something to do with Lettie. He tried to remember the last couple days, and all he saw was her tear-stained face. She had cried for him. Lettie had *cried* for him. No one had ever loved him enough to cry for him. More than that, Lettie was not a weak woman who resorted to waterworks. Her emotions humbled him.

Shane swallowed the lump in his throat. In his heart, he wanted to marry her, spend the rest of his life seeing her when he woke up every morning and went to sleep each night. He wanted to hear her order him around, grump when he didn't do what she asked, and most of all, he wanted to feel her in his arms. Right now.

When Karen came in with a plate of eggs and a biscuit, he managed to say thank you and eat dutifully as she watched. Although he couldn't finish the entire plate, he ate enough to satisfy whatever orders she had to make sure the food disappeared.

Karen was nice enough and took care of him, as everyone did at the Blue Plate. But he needed to see Lettie, and not only in his dreams. After Karen left, he fought against sleep, but in the end, it won.

Lettie went upstairs several hours after breakfast. There were no customers and no chores to be done. She'd been avoiding him. It was time to admit it to herself. She played childish games when what she really needed was to talk to him.

The best way to move forward was to stop standing still. It was time.

She walked up the stairs with purpose, ready to make a decision one way or the other. He might not remember asking her to marry him. That would be the worst of any situation she could imagine. The door to the room was closed, and she knocked softly.

"Come in." His voice sounded sleep-tinged, as though she had woken him.

Feeling a little guilty about disturbing his slumber, she opened the door wide enough to poke her head in. His face broke into a beautiful smile when he saw her.

"There's my girl."

Her heart jumped like a silly fool, and she found herself smiling back as she stepped into the room.

"Are you rested up? Mrs. Gunderson said you were here for two days straight." His expression was full of worry for her.

"I'm fine, but I wasn't shot. My legs are only bruised. They're healing up quick, mostly thanks to you taking care of me after the accident." She pulled the chair to the side of the bed and sat, her hands folded in her lap. Now that she was face-to-face with him, and he was fully alert, she found herself tongue-tied.

"Plus you were tied up and beaten by those bastards." His expression hardened. "I should have killed them for what they did."

She felt loved by his proclamation even if it was a bit bloodthirsty of him. "The law has them now. I expect they'll swing for their crimes."

"Did the Gundersons have to pay for the wagon?" He reminded her she had completely forgotten about the wagon, and the fact it was in pieces about twenty miles from town.

"I don't know. I should have asked, but I was worried about you." Her heart took over, pushing her overactive brain aside. "I thought I'd never talk to you again or kiss you or anything else with you. It about killed me, Shane. I didn't know what I'd do." She paused, frozen by her cowardice. Lettie gave herself a mental pinch. "I was scared."

He took her hand and kissed the back. "I didn't mean to worry you."

Her temper picked a terrible time to pop up. "Then you shouldn't have stepped in front of the bullet that was meant for me."

"I will take any bullet meant for you, over and over." He tugged her closer. "I meant it when I said I love you. That means I will do anything for you." His gray eyes were full of the one thing designed to turn her into a puddle.

Love.

"I ain't got a clue how to love nobody." Her voice shook, along with the rest of her. Now that they were out of danger, this was when the real words would be said.

He smiled and cupped her cheek. "Me neither. We can learn together. Marry me, Lettie Brown."

She turned her face so she could kiss his hand. "Are you sure?" Her question was barely above a whisper, every fiber of her body quivering with hope.

"I ain't been sure of much in my life, but I'm sure about this." He pressed his forehead to hers, and the warmth of his breath puffed across her lips. "Marry me."

She smiled, her heart and soul full of light and love. Lettie had finally found her home. "Yes."

The preparations for the wedding took over. Everyone was as busy for Lettie's nuptials as they had been for Angeline's months earlier. Lettie talked to more people and held entire conversations, more than she had all her life. Suddenly folks were seeing her as a town citizen and not as a temporary one.

Three weeks flew by in a blink. Each time she woke up, butterflies flitted around inside her as she thought of all the things that had to happen. They were getting married tomorrow, Saturday morning, at the restaurant, like Angeline and Sam. The Gundersons wouldn't hear of anything else.

Although Lettie wouldn't admit it, the attention made her feel special and loved. Two things she didn't know how to reciprocate. Soon she would learn, though, since she would have a husband by her side for the rest of her life. A real husband this time.

Lettie walked to Angeline's house after the dinner shift at the restaurant for the final fitting on her dress. It was a beautiful blue color, the same shade of the sky in winter. Angeline had insisted on it, telling Lettie she spent too much time in brown and assuring her that Shane would love it.

Her smile seemed permanently stuck to her face nowadays, much to Angeline's amusement. Lettie knocked on her friend's door and waited only two seconds before it flew open and a grinning Angeline stood there.

"You do not need to knock on my door. Get in here." She grabbed Lettie's arm and pulled her inside.

The next thirty minutes went by quickly, full of giggling and talking. Lettie felt so free, so light, so amazingly good. She reveled in the fact she was no longer living in darkness. A man's love and the strange dreams that bonded them together had brought her to this place.

"There, that's it, I think." Angeline stepped back, a smile on her pretty face. "Look in the mirror now."

Lettie didn't want to, since mirrors were not her friend, but she turned around. At first she kept her eyes closed, then slowly opened them. Standing in front of her was a woman she'd never seen before. She wore a beautiful sky-blue dress that hugged her curves, accentuating her full breasts and hips. Her hair was brushed to a sheen, lying in a thick braid on her shoulder. Her eyes sparkled in the sunlight streaming in from the right through the windows that faced the lake.

"I don't look like me," was what she managed to say.

"Oh yes you do. That's who you are hiding under all the brown." She whistled at Lettie's reflection. "It took falling in love to let the real you out."

Lettie wanted to hug herself, maybe pinch herself, to make sure it was real.

"You will be Mrs. Murphy tomorrow. No more brown or Brown."

The reminder of being Lettie Brown, second wife to Josiah Brown, felt like a bucket of cold water on her head. She'd told Shane almost everything except one small piece. A very important piece.

Her real name.

"Oh, Angeline, I'm in trouble." Her stomach clenched hard.

"What's wrong?" Angeline frowned, her expression full of confusion.

"I didn't tell him my real name. Oh my God, I *didn't tell him.*" Lettie's heart dropped to her feet.

"I don't understand. Your name isn't Lettie?" Angeline took her hands. "You're freezing cold."

Panic flooded her. "His wife, his first wife's name, was Violet. His daughter's name was Elizabeth. There were dreams and they were so real." Her words got all jumbled up inside. "Now he has to know who I am. I can't let him marry me unless he knows. The names are like poison to him though. What am I gonna do?"

Angeline led her to the kitchen table and pushed her into a chair. "I need to get you some coffee. You're not making any sense."

Lettie clutched her stomach and leaned forward. "I have to tell him, Angeline. I have to tell him my name."

"Lettie, what is your real name?" Angeline sat down, her golden brows together in a V.

"My name is Violet Elizabeth."

The sound of glass breaking echoed around them. Lettie started, and Angeline made a small squeaking noise.

Sam and Shane stood in the entrance to the kitchen. Her bridegroom's face was as white as the snow that surrounded the town in winter. On the floor in front of him lay the shards of a vase filled with blue wildflowers.

"What did you say?" His voice was barely audible.

"What's going on?" Sam looked as confused as Angeline.

"I don't know. She was smiling and laughing and then she started in about her real name." Angeline patted Lettie's hand. "I didn't know her name wasn't Lettie."

A sob burst from Lettie's throat as her happiness broke apart alongside the vase. "I'm sorry." She rose and walked toward him, her heart breaking at the pain in his face.

"What did you say?" he repeated, his voice now tinged with anger.

"My name." She swallowed the denial she wanted to throw at him. "My given name is Violet Elizabeth Stevens."

"I don't know you." Shane turned and left the kitchen, and took her heart with him.

Shane wandered for hours, the stitches in his stomach pulling and complaining about the overexertion after weeks of healing. He ignored the discomfort, ignored the strange looks from people when he didn't reply to their greetings.

Lettie's confession—no, *Violet's* confession—kept scraping across his mind like fingernails. She couldn't have a name like Mary or Edwina or Roberta. No, her name had to be *Violet Elizabeth.* And she'd kept it from him, knowing full well what the names meant to him.

She'd lied.

His heart hurt, aching with the slice of betrayal. She knew about his first wife. She knew his daughter had been murdered. She knew he'd done nothing to save them. Her very name mocked all of that.

Her name was *Violet Elizabeth.*

What kind of cruel God existed? Why would he put this woman in his path, make her feature in his dreams, have him fall in love with her? Why? When He knew the pain it would cause.

Shane wanted to forget the fact he knew she'd lied, that her name mocked his past. He wanted to marry her as planned and live the rest of his life in ignorance. Yet he couldn't. The wildflowers he'd picked so carefully for her bouquet swayed in the breeze in the field to his right. When he'd heard her dress was blue, he'd had to pick them for her.

Little had he known it would be the end of his dreams of Lettie.

It was as though his wife, Violet, laughed from the other side, pointing at him and cackling for his ineptitude as a husband and father, soldier and farmer. As if there could ever be salvation for a failure like him. The idea he would have married Lettie without knowing the truth made him sick. She deliberately hadn't told him.

He could understand why. If she wanted to snag herself a husband, not having the same name as his dead wife would be a good start. What he couldn't forgive was not telling him in the last three weeks. There had been plenty of opportunity. What would have happened when they signed the marriage certificate? Or when the preacher said her full name during the ceremony?

Shane was glad he'd found out now instead of when it was too late. He had thought Forestville would be the place he could reinvent himself. No one here knew Shane Murphy or the mess he'd made of his life in Missouri. Now they never would. He couldn't stay and see her every day. It would be too much.

Since he didn't have a single thing he owned, he could keep walking out of town, out of Wyoming, out of reach of her memory. The first Violet was a selfish, shallow woman who wanted to be pampered. The second Violet was a brave, strong woman who had beaten the odds to survive. She was also a liar.

Pain cut through him again, like tiny little knives slashing him to pieces inch by inch. Shane didn't know the town well enough to recognize where he wandered, but he found his boots in front of a saloon. His hands shook first, then his arms and soon his whole body trembled. Thirst roared through him, sinking its fangs into his heart.

Shane walked into the saloon.

Lettie wrung her hands and paced back and forth in the kitchen at Angeline's house. Her heart ached so hard it stole her breath. She'd hurt him badly, and he had walked away from her. Why oh why hadn't she told him weeks ago? Would it have made such an impact if she had?

She was sick with the knowledge she had lied to him by omission. There was no excuse for not telling him. If only she had said something before he'd told her the story of how he'd lost his family. But then he might not have told her, they might not have fallen in love, and they might not have planned on marrying.

Her lie made that all happen and now it tore it to pieces. Lettie threw herself in a chair and put her face in her hands, trying to breathe. Angeline walked up beside her and rubbed her back.

"Can you tell me what's wrong now? I've got Sam scouring the town for Shane, and neither one of us knows what happened." She squatted beside the chair and peered at Lettie beneath her arm. "I can't help you if you don't tell me."

Lettie blew out a shaky breath. "Part of it is his story and I can't do the telling for him. I can tell you that my real name, Violet Elizabeth, is powerful bad for him. I should have been honest, but I was afraid." Her voice wobbled with each word. "When the dreams started, I didn't know why or what would happen. Then I let myself love him."

"Dreams? I don't understand." Angeline pulled Lettie's hands away. "What dreams?"

Lettie's laugh was punctuated with a sob. "We both had dreams of each other, um, dreams about being together. You know, between the sheets and such. Vivid ones that was so real, I, um, woke up feeling them." She was embarrassed to admit she had woken up wet and aching for him.

Angeline, bless her heart, seemed to understand anyway. Her eyes widened. "Wait, both of you had these dreams? Were they the same dreams?"

"Uh-huh. Near as we can tell. We didn't talk about them second by second, but they were awful similar." She wiped her eyes with the already wilting handkerchief.

"How many dreams?"

"Four, I think. They started a few days after he got here." Lettie closed her eyes for a moment, remembering the intensity of the dreams and how real life taught her how muted the imaginings were. Being with him was better than anything she'd ever dreamed.

"Were they like memories?" Angeline seemed more than excited. Her expression lit up like a roaring fire.

"Yeah, they were like memories. Of course that's impossible because I ain't never met the man before. We sure as heck didn't do any of that before, well, before I had the dreams." Lettie didn't want to share too much detail with Angeline about what went on during the ill-fated supply trip. It was too personal, too painful.

"If I were my husband, I would say the spirits talked to both of you. Did you find a sparrow feather?"

Lettie was startled enough to forget about Sam. "How did you know?" She'd kept the feather in her chest of drawers. She'd considered throwing it outside but found she couldn't.

"Remember? I told you about Sam's mother." Angeline took Lettie's hands. "She was Indian, and her name was Sparrow. When Sam was courting me, I found a sparrow feather in the kitchen. I didn't know what to make of it until I found out about Sparrow. Her spirit looks after folks."

Lettie didn't pretend to understand any of it. "She doesn't know me. Why would she look after me? Is she a ghost?"

"No, she's not a ghost, and she doesn't have to know you. Sparrow is part of the spirit world, and they take care of all creatures on Earth." Angeline jumped to her feet. "I'm not doing a good job explaining this. We've got to find Sam and see if he found Shane."

They left the house and went in search of Angeline's husband. The sparrow feather was another strange piece of an already strange world she existed in. Thinking back, she'd seen a flock of sparrows, another feather on the printing press and yet another sparrow outside the cabin. It was all too much to be a coincidence. The idea Sam's dead mother was behind all those instances didn't scare her, but she didn't pretend to understand it. If Angeline thought Sparrow could help fix the mess with Shane, she wouldn't question it.

Shane was numb from his head to his feet, pleasantly numb. He could hardly put two thoughts together. In a twisted way, he'd missed drinking. The slow burn of the whiskey as it slid into his stomach. The buzz that spread outward from his gut to his head.

He stared at the amber liquid in the glass and licked his

lips. It would be his eighth drink, and he had only one more dollar to spend. Later on he'd be embarrassed he spent the five dollars Pieter had given him as a wedding gift. Now all he wanted was to sip at the drink and enjoy the smoky flavor.

The first three drinks had gone down too fast, and he barely tasted them. He'd slowed down and tried to sip the fourth, fifth and sixth, yet he'd found his glass empty before he knew it. But he'd been feeling good by then, real good. His pain had faded to a dull throb and then the seventh drink washed over that throb and the pain was gone.

He couldn't remember the last time he'd felt relaxed. Thank God there was a saloon in this town, whatever town it was. Something that started with an F, but it wasn't important. What he cared about was the next two drinks the final dollar in his pocket would buy.

Shane sipped the nectar, the flavor exploding in his mouth. Then in the blink of an eye, it was gone.

"Where did my drink go?" he heard somebody ask, and it echoed in his head. Shane glanced around and only saw the burly barkeep staring at him with a frown.

"You had enough, fella. I ain't serving you no more."

"I got a dollar left." He searched his pockets but didn't find any money. "Somebody took my money too."

The barkeep leaned over the bar. "You drank that money. It's in your gut."

Shane blinked. "I drank the money?"

"Ain't you one of the Gundersons' folk? I should go get Pieter." The man started to move when Shane grabbed his arm.

"Noooo, don't do that. He'll know I drank the money." Shane didn't know what it meant, but he knew Pieter couldn't know what he'd done.

"You can't stay here. Hell, I'm guessing you could drink a bottle of that cheap rotgut every hour if I gave it to you. Not here." The barkeep shook off Shane's grip easily. "You gotta leave. If you won't, then I'm gonna fetch Pieter."

Shane knew the familiar story, the boot in his ass when he ran out of money. He thought the town—Foresttown? Forestvalley?—was different somehow. The townsfolk had been nice to him and then there was somebody else. A woman.

Yes, a woman.

His stomach flipped upside down, spilling the whiskey. It burned like acid deep inside him. In a flash, he remembered exactly why he sat at the bar drinking his money away.

Lettie.

Oh God. Oh God. She wasn't Lettie. She was Violet Elizabeth. *Violet. Elizabeth.* The two names that would forever remind him of his failure as a man, a husband and a father. How could he love her? How could she love him and lie to him?

He laid his head down on the bar and waited for someone to drag him from the building and throw him in the dirt. His life wouldn't be worth a spit in the wind without Lettie anyway. He also couldn't be with her knowing her real name. It would be like rubbing salt in a wound every minute of every day.

He wasn't strong enough to get past it.

Tears stung his eyes as he fell back down to the bottom of life again. He was comfortable there, safe from the pain that waited for him.

"Shane?"

He lifted his head and spied a black-haired man standing beside him. "Hmm?"

"Oh hell, did you drink half a bottle of that shit?" The stranger put his arm around Shane's waist and hauled him to his feet. They made their way slowly to the door because the man had a hitch in his gait. "You could help by actually walking."

"I don't wanna go."

"You're going anyway. Mike doesn't want you in here. Angeline is going to kill me." The man sounded angry, but Shane didn't know who he was so it didn't matter, did it? "I didn't expect to find you here, so I wasted too much time looking every place else."

"Who are you?" Shane's head lolled back as he tried to look at the man. "Are you Indian?"

"Walk, Murphy. We're going to my house. I've got a surefire cure for that whiskey bath you took."

"I didn't take no bath. I drank the money Pieter gave me. Shhhh." Shane tried to put his finger on his lips but found it in his nose instead. "Don't tell him 'cause I don't want him to be mad."

The stranger's dark eyes held kindness and pity. "Ah, Murphy, you are a wreck."

Shane was used to pity but not the kindness. He was a leaf blowing on the wind, landing in puddles, mud and horse shit, never knowing who would step on him, break him into pieces or burn him. It was no way to live, but he didn't know any other.

A woman's voice sounded from the left. "What happened?"

"You don't want to know." The man kept half-dragging him down the street. Shane's feet hardly touched the ground.

"Oh my God. Has he been drinking?"

Lettie's voice cut through his whiskey haze like a sharp razor. Shane's head snapped up, and he spotted her wearing a blue dress the color of the sky, her brown gaze locked on him. At that moment, he wanted to hate her. He wanted to hate her so she couldn't ever hurt him again.

But he didn't and he couldn't. He wasn't strong enough, man enough for her. He tried to tell her to leave him in the puddle, but his words got tangled up. She came around to his other side and put her strong arm around his waist.

"I'm so sorry, Shane. So very sorry." Her voice was full of tears, regret and guilt. "I never wanted to hurt you."

"Not good enough" was what came out of his mouth. She stiffened, and he heard a little noise as though he'd kicked a kitten.

"I know I'm not, but that don't mean I don't love you."

"Noooo, not you. Me. I can't, shit, um." Dizziness swept over him, and sparks of light shot across his vision.

"We need to go to the house. Sam, I think your mother has had a hand in this. They've had identical dream memories of each other." The other woman sounded like she was in charge. "And Sparrow visited Lettie."

"What? When?" The man looked at Lettie. "Did she leave you a feather?"

Feather? How did they know about the feather?

"I don't know what it means, but I'm hoping it's good. There's been lots of sparrows lately." Lettie pressed her head against his. "It's not going to make him hate me any less."

"Have faith in the spirits, Lettie. They guided you here. They guided him here. You were meant to be together. We need to listen to them and find your path." The man was talking and the words should have made Shane's head hurt, but they didn't. They were clear as the night sky in summer. Something did bring him here, but he didn't know why. Was it for Lettie? Or was it for him? He fumbled with his pocket, elbowing the man unintentionally.

"What is he doing?" the blonde woman asked.

"I don't know. Fishing for something in his pocket." The man steadied him, and Shane was able to grasp what he was after. When he pulled out a sparrow feather, a few gasps sounded.

"Holy shit." Lettie was never a woman to shy away from cussing. "*He has a feather too.*"

Shane could see the blonde woman smiling widely. "Oh, Sam, the spirits talked to both of them. Sparrow did bring them together. We need to help them."

"Let's go to the lake. The spirits are strongest there. Perhaps they will speak to them." The man, yes his name was Sam, nodded at Lettie on the right, then headed down the road at a brisk pace. Good thing Lettie had long legs to keep up.

Memories crowded his mind of those beautiful long legs wrapped around his hips, creamy skin in the water, softer than any flower. "Your legs are beautiful."

Sam snorted. "I don't think he's talking to me."

The blonde walked in front of them, throwing worried glances back every few seconds. "We're almost there."

"What are we going to do when we get there?" Lettie was breathing hard, and it was because of him. She half-carried his sorry carcass.

"We're going to let the spirits guide you." Sam wasn't making much sense.

"But why the lake?" Lettie was persistent, and it made Shane grin. "What's special about it?"

"It's a spiritual place where nature and the spirits come together, where things are clearer. The spirits surround it, keep it safe. I'm hoping it will clean his head from the whiskey too." Sam grunted as they started walking up a small hill to the crest of the lake. "Angeline, can you bring coffee for Shane?"

Angeline, the blonde woman's name. She was Lettie's best friend and knew all her secrets. No, not all. Lettie had kept her real name to herself. That bitter truth poked him in the heart again.

"Yes, of course." Footsteps sounded in the leaves as presumably she went to retrieve the coffee.

Shane didn't want any. That would make the pain come back, take away the lovely haze he floated in. There were reasons he drank, and escaping was only one of them.

"Let's go to the grassy spot by the shore." Sam guided them down, the uneven ground making their progress slow.

"Sam, I still don't understand what I'm supposed to do." Lettie sounded desperate, exactly how he'd felt thirty minutes ago. She should have some whiskey too.

"Just let the spirits guide you, Lettie. They will show you the right path. I've found much of my own happiness here, and this is where I brought Angeline the first time we stepped out together." Sam stopped, breathing hard. "I see sparrows here all the time too. My mother is always around, keeping watch. She chose you two to help. Now you have to accept the help."

Sam and Lettie laid Shane down gently. He found himself lying on a soft bed of grass looking up at the puffy white clouds in the blue sky. It was almost the same color as Lettie's dress. She knelt beside him, her thick braid swaying dangerously close to his eye. She frowned, her brown eyes so full of pain he had to look away.

No, no, no. He didn't want to know he'd hurt her although he already knew he had.

"Shane. Look at me."

No, no, no.

"I'm sorry. I should have told you. I was afraid of losing you before I really had you." She took his hand in hers. He didn't pull away but he should have. It felt so good to touch her. That simple contact infused him with calm.

"Lied," came out of his mouth.

"I know. I lied. I love you, Shane. I ain't never loved anyone like this. I was scared." She squeezed his hand, and he realized hers were shaking. "Please don't hate me." Her voice had dropped to a raw whisper.

Sam had disappeared, leaving the two of them alone. A breeze picked up, and the sound of dry leaves dancing echoed across the water. The small hairs on his body stood at attention. His mind was suddenly clear as a bell. He pushed himself into a sitting position. Lettie knelt beside him, looking miserable and frightened.

"What's happening?"

She shook her head. "I don't know."

The breeze turned cold, then warm, winding its way around them. A hummingbird stopped directly in front of them, the hum from its wings sounding almost like a bee. It cocked its head and approached Lettie.

Her eyes widened as the bird seemed to examine her, then it flew close to him. As he stared at the beautiful green and yellow bird, it was as though it was studying him. In an instant, the bird flew away. Shane clutched the sparrow feather in his hand, his heart pounding hard enough to push the whiskey out of his pores in a rush.

Shane heard humming or chanting, low and distant. He looked at Lettie. "Do you hear that?"

"Someone's singing."

He glanced around at the empty lakeshore. "Who?"

"I don't know."

He studied Lettie kneeling beside him. The sight of her in the blue dress stole his breath. She looked just as he had imagined her, in the exact color to make his brown angel turn into a stunning vision. Her face was blotchy with tear stains, and her hair had escaped some of the thick braid. The wisps danced on her cheeks in the breeze.

Shane couldn't have explained it to anyone who asked, but he was no longer drunk, not even a little. Goose bumps danced across his skin as he stared at her. The chanting grew louder, his bones vibrating with each note.

He reached out and cupped her cheek. How could he have ever thought she was a wicked brown demon? Or a plain woman? She was exquisite, more beautiful than nature's bounty around him. Her heart was pure, and it beat for him as his beat for her.

"I'm sorry I didn't tell you about my real name."

"Your real name is Lettie."

She shook her head. "I would like it to be—"

"Then it is." Shane was crystal clear on what he needed to do. More clear than he'd ever been in his life. "We can leave behind who we were and be who we are."

She frowned, looking confused. "What do you mean?"

He put his hands on her shoulders and stared into her beloved brown eyes. "Sam was right about one thing. This lake cleared my head. I know now what I need. I love you. You love me. Who we were before a month ago, those people are dead and gone. I forgot that for a while because I was scared too."

Her frown disappeared, and hope blossomed in her expression. "You were scared?"

Shane managed a smile. "Of course I was. Once we're

married, I have to be a husband, a man. I ain't got a good history for either one of those. But I think we are like that bird, free to choose. I choose you. I choose *Lettie*."

Her smile was like the most beautiful sunrise he'd ever witnessed. "And I choose you. I choose Shane."

She threw herself into his arms. Shane hung on to her, her body melding with his into one being. The wind wrapped around them, the chanting grew louder still, vibrating through them, in them.

As they embraced, it was as though the spirits erased their sins, bathed them in forgiveness, and they were reborn. Their lives could begin again, together, without the burdens they had borne for so long.

The wind and the chanting stopped in a blink. They sat back and stared at each other for a moment. She looked as amazed as he was sure he did. His heart thumped steadily, full of hope for what lay ahead.

"Marry me, Lettie."

Her smile made his heart skip a beat. "I can't think of anything I want more."

This time when they kissed, it was soft, sweet and pure. A new beginning.

Chapter Nine

"You may kiss the bride." Will Barker, the young preacher who had settled in town less than a year ago, smiled at Shane. The minister's eyes sparkled as Lettie's new husband leaned in to kiss her.

His lips were soft and dry, the kiss barely a peck, but neither one of them wanted to put on a show for the folks attending the wedding. A whoop sounded from Sam and Sheriff Booth as the small group closed in for congratulations.

The men smacked Shane on the back while the women congratulated Lettie. It was a dream, one she hoped she never woke up from. Each of them had overcome the past that hung on their backs like anchors.

Lettie was almost full to bursting with pure joy. It radiated out from her heart through her entire body. She was nearly glowing like a star in the sky, shining bright. Shane's gaze fell on her as she was hugged for the fourth time by a weeping Marta. He waggled his eyebrows, and Lettie giggled.

She stopped and stared at him open-mouthed. She had *never* giggled in her life. Truthfully, she didn't know she could. Shane winked, and she giggled a second time. He pulled away from the men and hugged her hard. She wrapped her arms around his neck, and he swept her off her feet, twirling her in a circle.

Everyone laughed and clapped while he spun her in another circle. Lettie could feel the happiness in the air—it was almost visible. When he twirled her around for a third time, she pinched him.

"If you make me puke on you, I might not ever forgive you."

He buried his nose in her neck and laughed. "You'll never let me forget that I'm sure."

"No I'll tuck it away and use it when I need it." She laughed in his ear, earning a growl.

After another round of congratulations, the Gundersons served a feast for the small wedding party. It was a traditional German meal that looked delicious, but Lettie was too excited to eat much except for the strudel. That hit her sweet tooth but made her jitters worse.

Not only had she gotten married again, but she had another wedding night to get through. This one would be a pleasurable experience, unlike the first one. She pushed aside all thoughts of the nightmare that was her first lifetime. She was Lettie Murphy, for now and for always. The other woman she'd been no longer existed.

Their love and the magic of the lake had healed both of them, or perhaps it had been the sparrows.

While Shane chatted with the sheriff, Alice approached Lettie, a tentative smile on her face. For the first time since she'd met the young woman, Lettie smiled back.

"Congratulations." Alice gave Lettie's hand a small squeeze.

"Thank you, Alice."

Alice glanced down at her feet. "I don't know how to apologize for what happened with Buster. I didn't—"

Lettie cut her off. "You don't need to apologize. He is a son of a bitch who hurt both of us."

Alice shook her head. "He hurt you more. He tried to kill you and take everyone's money. All because I wasn't strong enough to fight him or keep my mouth shut." Misery laced her words.

Surprising herself, Lettie pulled Alice into a quick hug. "Like I said, he was a son of a bitch. What he did is his fault alone."

"You forgive me?" Alice looked impossibly young and hopeful.

"There's nothing to forgive, girl." Lettie gestured to the guests. "Now why don't you go get some vittles and enjoy the party?"

Alice smiled again, this time with genuine happiness. "I'm glad you found a man to love. Someday I hope to find my own."

With that, Alice turned away, leaving Lettie to wonder if the young woman would ever find what she sought. Not if she took to spending time with bastards like Buster and his cohorts. Maybe her friends could help that along.

Sam and Angeline appeared in front of her, big smiles on their faces and a paper-wrapped box in their hands. "We have a wedding present for you." Angeline handed the box to Lettie.

"We need Shane here too." Sam winked at his wife. "I'll be right back."

"What is it?" Lettie shook the small box, but it didn't reveal any secrets. She'd never received a gift before and found the anticipation was horrible. "Can I open it?"

"No, wait for Shane and Sam." Angeline laughed. "You'll like it, I promise."

Lettie didn't want to wait. She turned to the left and tried to untie the string without Angeline's notice.

"Now, now, don't cheat." Angeline tried to take the gift, but Lettie pulled it away. "Be patient, Mrs. Murphy."

Mrs. Murphy.

"That's the first time anyone's called me that." Lettie met

219

her friend's gaze, her throat tight with emotion. "It's the first time I'm happy to be who I am."

Angeline pulled her into a tight hug, and Lettie was glad to return the embrace. Another first for her. Physical affection hadn't been enjoyable or wanted. Now things were different. She was different.

"Oh my." Angeline pulled back. "That had to be the longest hug we've ever shared."

Lettie took her friend's hands and squeezed. Angeline had been the one constant in her life since she had married Josiah Brown. Impossible they'd escaped after a mere two months, yet were closer than most siblings. They survived the worst and emerged on the other side of darkness together. Angeline was the best friend anyone could ever want. "Thank you for not giving up on me."

"I would never do that." Angeline cocked her head to the left. "You are, and always will be, my friend. I love you, Lettie, no matter what."

Lettie nodded, too overcome with emotion to respond in kind. She hoped one day she could tell her friend how much she meant to her, but Angeline understood. She always had. Life had stopped kicking Lettie and gifted her with all she could ever want.

"Now give me that gift back before you open it," Angeline teased.

"I'll think about it."

They both laughed, lost in the friendship that had defined them as women. The men returned and found them nearly in tears from laughing so hard. Happiness had come to stay, and Lettie reveled in the experience. Never again would she live in the darkness.

"Now you can open it." Angeline pointed to the box. "We

hope you like it."

Shane raised his brows and watched Lettie as she untied the twine with trembling fingers. When she finally got the box open, a folded piece of paper and a key were inside.

Lettie frowned at her friends. "What is it?"

"Read it."

Shane took the paper and unfolded it. "It's a deed." His eyes widened as he looked at Lettie. "It's a deed to a house in both our names."

"House? What house?" Lettie held the key in her hand and wondered why it looked familiar.

"Your house, silly goose. The house you've been living in." Angeline looked as though she'd burst from grinning. "Both of us decided you deserved a home, and what better place than the house that brought Sparrow into your lives, and to each other."

Lettie was speechless. She thought she'd been emotional before, but this was too much. Shane watched her, waiting for her to respond. He respected her, which was a unique experience but one she could get used to.

"I-I don't know what to say."

Shane grinned. "Say thank you."

"It's too much. I can't take your house." Lettie couldn't imagine giving anyone a *house* as a gift.

"It's not our house. We have a house down by the lake. That was my father's house. I know he and my mother would love for you to live there, raise your children, be happy and enjoy every moment as much as they did." Sam folded the key into her palm. "Please take it."

She met Shane's gaze and saw the absolute love there. Life had given her so much already, and now it had given her a home of her own to share with the man she loved, her husband.

Lettie turned back to Sam and Angeline. "Thank you."

They both grinned and went back to the food, hand in hand. Lettie stood there, trembling and overwhelmed with the bounty she now had. Shane wrapped his arms around her and held her tight, his heart beating against hers in a steady rhythm.

"I love you, Shane Murphy."

He sighed softly. "And I love you, Lettie Murphy."

She closed her eyes and breathed in his familiar scent. The brown bird had transformed into a hummingbird, flying free into the blue sky of life, her mate at her side. Love had saved them, love would embrace them, love would be the foundation for their home and if they were truly blessed, cradle their children.

Darkness into light.

About the Author

Beth Williamson, who also writes as Emma Lang, is an award-winning, bestselling author of both historical and contemporary romances. Her books range from sensual to scorching hot. She is a Career Achievement Award Nominee in Erotic Romance by *RT Book Reviews*, in both 2009 and 2010.

Beth has always been a dreamer, never able to escape her imagination. It led her to the craft of writing romance novels. She's passionate about purple, books and her family. She has a weakness for shoes and purses, as well as bookstores. Her path in life has taken several right turns, but she's been with the man of her dreams for more than twenty years.

Beth works full-time and writes romance novels evening, weekends, early mornings and whenever there is a break in the madness. She is compassionate, funny, a bit reserved at times, tenacious and a little quirky. Her cowboys and western romances speak of a bygone era, bringing her readers to an age where men were honest, hard and packing heat. For a change of pace, she also dives into some smokin' hot contemporaries, bringing you heat, romance and snappy dialogue.

Life might be chaotic, as life usually is, but Beth always keeps a smile on her face, a song in her heart and a cowboy on her mind.

To learn more about Beth Williamson, please visit www.bethwilliamson.com or send an email to Beth at beth@bethwilliamson.com.

PUBLISHING

It's all about the story...

Romance

HORROR

www.samhainpublishing.com

CPSIA information can be obtained at www.ICGtesting.com
Printed in the USA
BVOW080839070313

314963BV00002B/5/P